BETWEEN
WAS
and
WILL BE

BETWEEN WAS and WILL BE

Stories

Welton Rotz

TC Publishing
San Francisco

Between Was and Will Be/Welton Rotz
ISBN: 979-8-218-66118-2

To Barbara
In dialogue as usual

TALKING STONES Black granite, each approx. 36" tall

CONTENTS

INTRODUCTION

The time and space between what was and what will be.
The past is finished. The future hasn't emerged. Now what?
This is the liminal space. The betwixt and between.

I had no intention for my third book to have a theme. But as my creative muse developed words on the page, a common thread appeared, woven through some of the stories. I, we, my characters are scrambling and searching through this unfamiliar liminal space.

Will we ever arrive?

Will we ever know what will be?

JUST DO IT

"Ain't nothin' to it, but to do it"
Attributed to both Maya Angelou and Ronnie Coleman

It's easy to say "Ain't nothin' to it." But often not so easy "to do it." I can remember now, with a clarity that brings a shiver up my back and the hairs on my arms standing on end, when I first confronted the determination needed "to do it."

I lived on my Cal 32, in Sausalito, California. Moorage was cheaper than an apartment, a necessity now that I was divorced. At 33, life was ahead of me, including a new lady. A popular song, *"If I were a carpenter, would you marry me anyway?"* was on the air waves. Everything demanded my time: my construction job, my new relationship, and most important, weekend visits with my young daughter. There was no time to sail.

1

What is the value of living on a sailboat if you don't sail? The space is too small, personal hygiene is limited, and the confines can become claustrophobic. Commitments were tearing me apart. I felt pressure from every compass point. How does one set a course when each direction takes so much? Where is ME in all this? I knew that sailing was the healing balm for my torn wounds. It had been so for the past twenty-three years, since I had learned to sail at the age of ten. I also knew the painful emptiness of not sailing, living on the great plains of western Kansas, no sizable body of water and no boat. It was time to integrate the healing joy of sailing. It was time "to do it."

Making major changes in life can be terrifying. I can still feel the fear in those days and nights, trying to decide. What had to be given up? Where to steal the time?

When I finally set my course, it was easier than I had feared. In the late afternoons I was tired, coming home from a hard day's work. But every morning, I made my bed and cleaned up before I left for work. My boat was ready to sail. It had a reliable diesel engine and roller reefing on both main and head sails. Starting the engine, disconnecting the shore power cord, and throwing off the mooring lines, I was effortlessly underway in five minutes.

Sometimes I sailed for only twenty or thirty minutes. That was long enough to find the ME. I sailed or motored every day rain or shine, except in the very worst of storms. I enjoyed going out in the rain, feeling the drops on my face, and even the chills up my back. I felt alive again, one hand on the tiller, the other on the sheet. The installation of a wood-burning ship's stove made the cabin very cozy and dry. It fit perfectly in the galley space, the smoke pipe exiting up through a Charlie Noble. My daughter and my new lady often joined me on weekends. The small built-in bunk gave my daughter her own space when visiting. I experienced an exuberance of happiness, no longer feeling I had to steal time for myself.

Fifty years later, with my white beard and hair, I'm sometimes accused of being Santa spending the off-season in sunny California. Even if I were Santa, I'm confined to a wheelchair. I miss sailing. I also miss driving. But having lived through that difficult transition with my grandpa, and then experiencing my own father's rage when we took away his car keys, my decision has been relatively easy. In some ways, no longer driving is a relief.

But sailing is different, it's been a core element in my life for so very long. Growing old, giving away, giving in, and giving up seems to be a part of the greater scheme of life. (Although I am still with the lady I met fifty years ago) However, I do have the memories: the sails catching the wind and the boat coming alive. And that aliveness surging through my body giving me inner joy.

I'm an old codger now. I offer a simple bit of advice: go sailing (or motoring) as often as you can. You will be happy you did, both now and in your future.

Just Do It

DAN'S FEAR

He was doing pushups in the middle of the steep hiking trail. By the time I scrambled down to him, he was starting to stand up. His body glistened in the warm sunlight, sparkling from the sheen of sweat on his shirtless torso. He looked like one of those Greek gods rising out of something.

I asked if he was okay, and why he was doing pushups in the middle of a hiking trail on Mt. Tam. We introduced ourselves. With difficulty, he pulled a wrinkled business card from his jeans pocket. It said: Dan's Construction, with a local Sausalito phone number.

We started down the trail together. He was limping.

"Must have twisted my ankle," said Dan, "There was a patch of loose stones. I'm alright."

Again, I asked him why he was doing pushups on a hiking trail.

"It's part of an exercise program I'm doing. I run uphill as fast as I can…until my legs give out. Then do as many crunches as I can. I roll over and do pushups until my arms say 'Enough!'"

"But why?" I asked again.

"I'm strengthening my body," he replied. "I want to be prepared for an emergency."

"But—"

"I'm rarely afraid," said Dan. "But there was this one terrifying incident…" His voice trailed off. We walked on in silence. Breathing deeply, Dan began his story.

A caller had said he wanted a "builder" to look at a project at his home in Sausalito. Dan did not have a contractor's license yet, so it was technically illegal for him to operate as a contractor, unless the homeowner signed the building permit as "contractor" for the job.

But work was work.

Dan parked on the street. The owner's expensive sports car took up most of the parking apron. The home was built out from the side of the hill and held up by tall posts. Dan noticed a two-inch gap between the concrete parking slab and the turn-in slab from the street. Not good: any rainwater running off the street would flow down into the crack and erode the foundation below.

The front door opened directly into the home which was one large room with windows on three sides. In the center was a huge, majestic stone fireplace.

"I built it myself," said the owner. "Brought down stones from rivers in the Sierras. Phew! They're heavy!"

Dan could imagine, some were larger than basketballs.

The owner was smiling. He walked over and proudly caressed the beautiful, water-polished trophies.

Stone weighs about 200 pounds per cubic foot, that's 12 x 12 x 12 inches. The stones were laid from floor to ceiling, with copious amounts of concrete mortar to hold the puzzle together.

In the reflected light from the windows, the floor appeared to undulate. It was not level. This was wrong.

"Oh, by the way, can you fix that window? It's stuck, seems the frame is wacko," said the owner. "As you can see, there's limited space. I want you to build me a room below the house"

Dan asked if he had a set of plans and a permit.

"Hell no!" the owner replied. "You'll be working out of sight."

Dan knew he would be in violation, no license and no permit. And the building department in Sausalito was very tough to work with. But work was work.

He and the owner slipped and slid down the side of the house, through poison oak and wild blackberries, thorns snagging their pant legs all the way to the last support. Dan settled his feet and studied the post. Something was wrong. The concrete footing that anchored the timber had moved. It was tipped slightly downhill, kicking the tall post out of plumb.

Dan turned to me on the trail, his face ashen. "My body, my psyche reacted. A cold shiver slammed through my body. This was not good. My eyes searched up, under the floor of the house looming over us. I began to sweat, a cold sweat. My eyes focused on the main beam of the house, stretching from one side to the other, supporting all the floor joists, carrying the whole load of the floor above."

Dan's hands were shaking. He stopped, took some deep breaths. "Under the house..." He stopped again, exhaled with a groan, then continued. "The main timber was constructed from six, two-by-twelves set side-by-side on edge, making a nine-by-eleven-and-a-half-inch beam. It had begun to roll over. The beam was failing!"

"Oh my god!" I said.

"Yeah!" Dan nodded. "The compact stack of boards was slipping apart, disintegrating, separating. The bottom edge of the outside two by twelve-inch plank, the one carrying the greatest load, was splintering, breaking! The grain of the wood, the very fibers were splitting out as the beam bowed down from the weight above. The image of the immense stone fireplace just above me slammed into my mind. I couldn't speak, just started to shake. I wanted to run, but my legs didn't work, they just wobbled. This was not a question of 'flight or fight.' I had to get away. Flight was the only way to survive.

"I looked up the slope, my only escape route, and my legs started to move. My hands reached out, pulling me up, helping me climb. I tried not to grab poison oak. My jeans felt very tight. They were wet; I had peed myself. The owner's shouts followed me up to the street.

"Sitting in my truck, I was trying to recover my breath, but I was shaking too violently to even put the key in the ignition. The owner appeared at my window. He shouted, 'What the hell!' and gripped my window. 'Where are you going?'

"The truck was shaking. Was it his hands on the window or my adrenaline?

"'Your house,' I barely managed to say, 'is about to fall down—'
'The hell it is!' the owner yelled.

"I wanted to explain the situation, offer helpful suggestions, but the owner would not listen. He continued to shout and shake the truck.

"I managed to get the key in the ignition and start the truck.
'Ah, go to hell!' the owner shouted."

"Clutching the steering wheel, it was red with blood. My hands hurt. Opening my fingers, my palms were a mass of deep scratches from frantically grabbing blackberry vines. I started the truck and drove away."

Dan let out a big sigh.

I looked with new understanding at the bandages on his hands.

We walked down the trail in silence.

GOT AWAY WITH IT

All along the California coast where the bluffs meet the ocean, the land has been slipping and sliding into the Pacific taking large chunks of the coastal highway with it. Slide Ranch had been a productive dairy farm until too much pasture was lost to the ever-hungry waves.

In the mid-1960s, a band of hippies moved into the farm's few remaining buildings. They posted "Keep Out" signs and hung a chain (unlocked) across the road.

A friend of theirs, Stan, invited me to go abalone diving among the boulders, just off the shore. And yes, abalone diving was illegal…it was poaching.

I had met Stan while working with a salvage dive company in the Caribbean. I was recovering from a painful divorce. Stan and I became friends working side by side on numerous projects over a year. After earning my trust, he told me that he was on the dive job "laying low," hiding from the law because of some 'monkey business' he had done.

Slide Ranch was a good spot for abalone poaching, no one dared invade the hippy inhabitants. On a beautiful, sunny day, Stan and I drove past the tumbled-down farm structures to the end of the road, just above the bluff. He backed his truck into the only available space, next to a bright green VW Bug. It was also parked for a quick exit.

Stan carried one duffel bag with a spear gun, both of our wetsuits, face masks, snorkels, and rubber flippers. My bag held dive knives, ab tools, and clinking bottles of something. I had done a lot of spearfishing, but diving for abalone would be a new, exciting experience.

We slipped and slid down to the water. Quickly dressing in our dive gear, Stan checked to see if I was fitted correctly.

"It's pretty murky out there, and a lot of current," he said. "Don't feel around a rock to find an ab, and don't ever grab an ab still stuck on a rock."

"Why not?" I asked.

"Ha!" he said. "It'll clamp down faster than you can move. Then you'll have to cut off your finger to come up for air."

"Okay," I answered with newfound apprehension.

It was a challenge wearing flippers to walk over the slippery rocks from the shore into the cold Pacific Ocean. The water was murky, and the fierce current tried to knock me down. Not anything like diving in the liquid crystal-clear water of the Caribbean.

Once out into deep water, the profound beauty surrounded and captivated me. Tall seaweed danced sensuously in the current. The long leaves seemed to beckon me forward to join them. The brown-green fronds embraced me, then let go, not holding me back, allowing other stands to caress my body. It was easy to swim through this forest being touched on my face, my arms, and between my legs. For a moment, I had to repress the desire to strip off my dive suit and enjoy the sensuous touching with my bare skin. Fortunately, a trickle of cold water found its way into my neoprene suit and down my back.

A fish, a good-sized fish glided past, occasionally taking a bite of something on one of the seaweed branches. These blades were alive, so vastly different from the ugly, fly-infested brown-black shriveled seaweed thrown up on a beach after a storm at sea. My forest parted and I confronted a large boulder. A huge abalone was growing on its side. Everything underwater is magnified about 20%, but still, this was a magnificent find. I couldn't hold my breath any longer.

I hurried to the surface to fill my lungs. Stan was nowhere to be seen. Returning down to my bountiful boulder, I harvested the big prize and another abalone, slipping them into my getter bag. Resurfacing again, I saw Stan already climbing out of the water and unto the rocky shore.

"I got three," he called out as I groped my way ashore through the slippery rocks. "How many you got?"

"Two."

"Good, that's enough for the day," he said. "I got a fish, too."

We left the getter bags and abalone in the water by the shore. Stan brought up the fish. It was a blue lingcod, one of my favorite, only found in the kelp beds near the California coast.

We unzipped the tops of our tight wetsuits, and let the arms dangle. Stan explained how we would prep the meal. Build a fire between two or three rocks, and let it die down to hot coals. Meanwhile, we would pry out the large foot muscle of the abalone, make thin slices, and pound them with a rock until they were tender and even thinner. The steaks would cook in the cleaned shell.

"There are some old shells around," I said. "Should I pick up one?"

"No, we'll use the abs' own shell, tastes better."

We built the fire. Stan went around a huge boulder to look for more firewood, about 30 feet away. He came back with a big grin on his face.

"There's a couple screwing like crazy over there," he said. "Didn't see me."

We heard a door slam above in the parking area. A man wearing a uniform slipped and slid down the bank.

"Oh, shit!" said Stan. "The fish cops." He ran around the boulder again, but returned in a flash with an even bigger grin.

"I told them the cops were coming and they had to get out of here," Stan said. "The girl must have been underage; they took off like a bat outta hell. Didn't even get dressed, just their shoes."

We continued tending the fire, adding small sticks to build up the coals, never looking up.

"Hey you," came a voice from the rocks, a few feet above. "Police." The man stumbled down closer. He had drawn his gun and was shaking it at us.

We stood up, and the tops of our dive suits fell to the back. Bare-chested, our arms down, we held our fingers splayed open, palms facing the gun.

Stan took a half step forward and said, "Put your gun away! We've done nothing wrong."

It worked. It was the first time I had heard 'the voice' used.

"Fish 'n Game," said the officer, replacing his gun in its holster. "You've been poaching abalone."

"No, sir," said Stan. "We're just fishing." He gestured to our large fish lying near the fire.

"Do you have a fishing license?"

"Yep," replied Stan. "Up in my truck,"

"It was reported that two guys were diving for abs."

"Yeah," said Stan, pointing out to the water. "When we got here there were two divers. Did you see a green, or was it blue, hmm, VW Bug up there?"

From above came the rattle-roar of a VW starting, and the urgent sound of wheels throwing gravel.

"Yep, that must have been them. When they saw you coming, they dropped their getter bags in the water and took off like a rat chased by a cat. Guess they didn't want to get caught with incriminating evidence."

"Damn it!" shouted the officer.

"Yep," said Stan. "Do you want me to free those poor abs? I still have my dive suit on and I could take them out and set them on a rock."

"Yeah, I guess so."

Stan zipped up his suit and looked for the getter bags.

"How many in the bags?" the officer asked.

"Looks like four, no, five total," said Stan. "I'll go out and put them on a rock. They'll live." To me, he said, "Keep the fire going, We need hot coals for the fish."

I busied myself with the fire. When Stan was out of hearing, the officer asked me if I had ever dove here before.

"Nope, and never again. It was too cold, too murky, and too much surge."

"Do you know Stan?" asked the officer. I was surprised he knew Stan's name.

"Not really, first time diving with him," I answered.

"You know," said the officer, "we've been trying to catch him for months. You best stay away from him."

Stan returned. "Mission accomplished. Are the coals ready?" He pulled out his very large dive knife and began sharpening a stick to skewer the fish. A very primitive and inefficient way to cook. "Officer, would you like to join us eating this beautiful fish?"

"Thanks, but I gotta be on my way."

As he climbed up the rock slide, he turned. We gave a friendly wave.

With a satisfying smile, Stan said, "Ok, let's do this right.

Take out the items for cooking from your duffel. I'll fillet this magnificent fish. The coals are about ready."

I opened the bag and found a roll of aluminum foil, paper plates, forks, paper towels, small bottles of olive oil and vinegar, salt and pepper, two sourdough rolls, two small glasses, a Meyer lemon, and a half bottle of a good California white wine.

Stan seasoned the fillets, wrapped them in foil, and laid them in the coals.

"You know," said Stan after tasting the fish. "I think this is better than any abalone I've eaten."

"I wouldn't know," I said. "I've never tried ab, but this is the best!"

"Yep."

"That was quite a job you did on the fish cop." Looking up the bank, I added, "You really sold him a sack of sh—"

"Yeah, I could sell most anything, to anyone."

We both laughed.

A few weeks later, I got a call from Stan. He asked if I wanted to do some 'monkey business' with him. No mention of what it was. I told him I was in a new relationship, doing well, and did not want to run the risk of messing it up. He said he understood, his girlfriend was pregnant and that changed everything. Her mother was not happy, so they were going to LA. Maybe get married and even get a job.

We talked for a bit. "I'm happy to have known you," he said.

I said, "Me too, keep in touch."

Two or three years later, I received a note from Stan, written on letterhead from a major auto dealership. He was excited about being the father of the most beautiful, sweetest boy ever seen. He and the mother had gotten married before the birth. He had changed his name to hers. This made the "grandma" very happy.

Stan said he was now the vice president for used vehicle sales at the prestigious dealership. His final words were, "I really enjoy selling cars."

IT WAS NICE

"It was nice sleeping with you."

That's what he said, just like that. Neither of us had said anything, before or after. He sat up from the long bench facing mine, and put the book he'd been using as a pillow in his backpack. Looking at me, he smiled and said, "It was nice sleeping with you." I wondered what he was reading. Standing up, he moved forward to join the line departing the ferry.

I don't feel so good. It's been a long ride across Puget Sound from Seattle to Bainbridge Island. I'd better use the restroom before I get off. I wonder if I've started my period. It's late, very late.

When I told Joe, he just got mad. Said to get rid of it. Didn't discuss it, didn't offer to marry me. We've been living together since graduation. Joe wanted me to pay half the rent on his place. Waiting on tables gave me some money, but long hours. I was always tired. Just wanted to sleep. He was usually conked out when I got home after a double shift. I tried to be quiet when I came to bed, but he rolled over on top, got his rocks off, and went back to sleep.

There's a knock on the bathroom door. "Excuse me miss. You have to depart the ferry. Even if you're a round-trip passenger, you still have to get off and then re-board."

"I'm coming, just a minute."

The walk to long-term parking gives me time to think. Relieved I used the restroom. That's one problem taken care of. Guess I'm a little afraid to go home. So many problems there.

I'm glad I went to visit my friend Amy in Seattle. Gave my body time to decide what it was going to do. We've been friends since 6th grade, but I wonder if what she said makes any sense. All that BS about creating one's reality. No way would I have created this mess, this life with Joe. I hoped we'd get married someday. Nope!

After graduation, Amy moved to Seattle and I moved in with Joe. Guess I'm a little envious, everything seems to work out for her. She has a good job, a nice apartment, takes classes at the junior college, and still has time for friends.

My car's door handle is very warm. The sun is shining, that beautiful Pacific Northwest light. The sky was overcast in Seattle, not cloudy, just a grayness. Opening the windows, letting the car cool off. I'm feeling some apprehension about returning home. I just sit here. All around me is beauty. The sunlight dancing on the waters of Puget Sound. The rich greens of the forest embrace me. And to the south, majestic snowcapped Mount Rainer fills the horizon.

The library book I thought I might need is on the seat beside me. The librarian looked at me and raised her eyebrows.

"No," I said quickly, "I have a friend, in Seattle, I'm going to visit her, she's pregnant, needs help picking out a name."

Opening the book, "Amy" was on the first page.

"The name Amy holds a profound spiritual meaning that encompasses the qualities of compassion, nurturing, and being beloved. In a spiritual context, Amy represents an individual who possesses a deep sense of empathy and understanding towards others." —The Bump.

Hum, maybe Amy was onto something. She said, "Of course, you didn't create a life of discomfort with Joe directly. It was a string of decisions, moment by moment."

Like how I kept having sex with him, again and again even though it was not satisfying or loving. Moving into his place, with the fantasy of getting married. Going along with his lifestyle, not mine. Again and again, decisions, large and small, building my reality.

I have to let this sink in. Amy also said that we each have a spirit guide that helps us through life. Often, scenarios are set up for us to interact with, thus creating our reality at that moment. She said that it was important to say, "thank you," giving recognition to that guidance.

I smile, remembering my "sleeping partner" on the ferry. His face, after he fell asleep. So peaceful, so gentle, so beautiful. Sleeping together had been enjoyable, nurturing even without sex. There was a glow around him and I was inside that glow. I felt it. I want to create a man, a partner, like him. I could have jumped up and ran after him. But maybe I was not yet ready to accept that I could make conscious decisions.

There is work to be done. All around me is the beauty of the Pacific Northwest, a good place to start. First, clear out all my stuff from Joe's apartment. Then…build a new reality.

Starting my car, I feel a little giddy; frightened, excited, happy, all while sensing some of that stranger's glow around me.

"Thanks," I say. "It was nice."

LOCKS

"Hey Eric, you're right. There is a boat down there."

Jeff looks up and sees a man standing about 20 feet above him, looking down from the concrete edge of the lock.

"Hang in there," says the man. "We'll give you a lift in a moment. You tied okay?"

Jeff checks his lines again and adjusts the protective fenders for a better fit to the floating side wall of the lock. His 18-foot Mercury sailboat is dwarfed in the cavernous chamber. It's the bottom of the tide and the boat's mast protrudes only a foot above the top edge, almost invisible to the lock master.

Maybe I should install a mast headlight, Jeff thinks. *I do like sailing at night.*

On Seattle's Lake Union, the gentle evening breezes, the city lights marching right down to water's edge, the sparkling dance continuing their reflection on the lake create a perfect setting for sailing. Sometimes, from his north shore moorage, the moonrise paves a silver path across the lake. A path Jeff enjoys exploring. He often feels he could continue sailing all the way to the moon.

The lock gates close behind him, and the water in the chamber begins to rise to meet the level of the Seattle ship channel. The massive gates looming up before him, holding back a 20-foot wall of water, leak a constant swish splashing just ahead. It's a reminder of the awesome power they restrain, all the way back through the ship channel and Lake Union, and through the Montlake Cut into Lake Washington. Seattle's Ballard locks are an engineering marvel from 1917.

As the water level rises, Jeff recalls his first venture returning through the locks. It was a busy weekend afternoon. The lock master had ordered Jeff to proceed to the head of the crowd of boats and to tie alongside a larger, powerful diesel inboard cruiser. He passed over a bow line and a stern line. The fenders were already set. This tie-up put Jeff the distance of three boats out from the lock wall, almost in the center of the chamber. He had seen and felt hostile looks from some impatient boaters positioned farther back. But this was where he had been directed to tie.

Just as now, Jeff was only a few feet back from the massive gate. As the water level began to rise, so did the tension in the lock. It seemed like every boat engine was running. Soon, the confined space inside the lock filled with engine exhaust. Breathing became unpleasant. Everyone wanted to get out.

The large gates slowly opened to the ship canal. Engines were revved. Before the gates opened completely, the tie-to boat threw off Jeff's bow and stern lines. Gunning their engine, they shot out through the opening gates. The backwash from the boat's propeller pushed Jeff back into the now moving pack of boats. He knew he had to bring in the two mooring lines before they tangled in his propeller.

Jeff pushed the throttle lever on his small outboard engine against the peg. The engine howled, but the little boat could not keep ahead of the charging powerboats pressing him from behind. Jeff maneuvered his way to the side of the mass of boats. Taking a chance, he had set a course just outside the channel markers. There was plenty of water under his keel.

Jeff's memory fades. The water levels off, and the gates slowly move, the lock opens.

"Nice looking boat," says the lock attendant who is now almost level with Jeff. "Have a great evening. Going far?"

"Lake Union, not bad," says Jeff starting his outboard motor.

There is no dependable wind in the ship channel, plus Jeff wants to get home. He sets the outboard's throttle at ¾, not as fast as possible but easier on the ears. It will be about forty-five minutes to his moorage.

I wish I had a boat with a cabin, thinks Jeff. *I'd love to sleep on the boat tonight. Well, that's just how this whole day's scenario began.*

Jeff loved his 18-foot Mercury, painted Hunter Green with red mahogany brightwork. The Egyptian cotton sails were soft and felt good to the touch when taken down and stowed. They took extra care, but he had hooks in his basement to hang the sail if it got wet, a frequent reality in Seattle. One hook under the stairs, one next to the back door, and one above the small window. The room could still be used with the sail hanging high to dry.

But like many of us, Jeff got the "Two Foot Disease." You know, wanting a boat just a little bigger, preferably one with a cabin and a bunk. He started looking at sailboat ads in the paper and on postings at chandleries. Jeff noticed an ad for a 21-foot double-ended, gaff-rigged cutter. The price was out of his reach. After a few months, the ad reappeared. This time the price had been lowered and the ad included a photo of the boat under sail.

What a beauty! The hull was black, with white topsides. The gaff main sail appeared to be pulling well, and Jeff noticed that there were three rows of reef points. The cutter rig had two head sails: one rigged on the bowsprit, the other attached to the bow stem. The white cabin sported two fore and aft oval ports. In all, very salty. Jeff had never sailed a gaff rig, but he was captivated by the eye-catching "traditional" appearance. Looking closely at the photo, Jeff wondered if the pipe coming out of the cabin top was a chimney for a stove, or cabin heater protruding through a Charlie Noble.

The lowered price was almost within reach. Jeff's mind began to race, looking for a way to make this his boat. Perhaps, at least, he could look at the boat. The phone number listed was an answering service. Jeff left a message suggesting a meeting next Saturday. His call was answered within a few minutes.

"Yes, the boat was still for sale.

Yes, Saturday was good.

The boat was located in Winslow, across Puget Sound from Seattle. Was that a problem?

Meet at the coffee shop near the public dock and ferry?

About one o'clock.

You may want to purchase a one-way ferry ride. Ha ha!

You may want to sail it home.

Bring your checkbook."

Jeff remembered the ad had indicated "Sail Away Price"

Maybe they were just motivated sellers

"Oh, you're sailing over? GREAT! Maybe work a trade.

See you Saturday. Same time, same place.
'Bye."

Click

Jeff cast off at first light Saturday morning. He planned to explore Bainbridge Island if he arrived early. A stiff breeze carried him to the Ballard Locks more quickly than expected. The larger of the two locks was filling with small and medium-sized boats, mostly fishermen eager to hit the salmon in the Sound. He wondered if he would have to take in a reef out in the open water. Stowing his sails, setting out fenders, and starting the outboard, Jeff entered the lock. With all the small boat traffic, he was relieved to have arrived at the locks as soon as he had.

Leaving the locks under power, he motored out to salt water. With the fresh wind on the Sound, Jeff made the whole voyage to Winslow on one tack. Holding the slight weather helm with one hand on the tiller, the mainsail sheet in the other, Jeff felt his power. The power of controlling the two great fluids of the earth: the winds and the waters.

The crossing took only two and a half hours. Arriving earlier than planned, Jeff explored the area around Bainbridge Island. Returning along the East shoreline, he thought he could make out in the distance the black and white colors of "his" boat entering the Winslow harbor. Jeff hove to, allowing the Washington State Ferry to maneuver out of the ferry dock. This was the ferry he would have taken. Approaching the guest dock, he could make out an attractive woman standing by an empty mooring space.

Sailing towards the space, he dropped his sails, and as the boat slowed, he came to rest at the dock in front of the woman.

"Hi, are you Jeff? I'm Mary. Nice move."

He nodded, tossed her the bow line as he stepped off, and cleated the stern line. Going forward, Jeff checked the fenders, checked the bow line Mary had cleated, and added a spring line.

Jeff completed securing his boat and looked at Mary. "Thanks for saving me a dock space."

She smiled.

"Glad you could come. The boat is at the far end of the dock. My boyfriend is there."

Jeff returned her smile and said, "Let's go." But stood for a moment taking in her appearance.

She was attractive, late 30s or 40s, although Jeff knew he had difficulty determining a woman's age. Maybe 50s. Her outfit was a pair of blue jeans, way too small and too tight. And a boy's work shirt, also too small. The top two buttons were left open, revealing her cleavage, The third button was almost out of its buttonhole, straining to hold the rest of her in place.

"*Hummm,*" thought Jeff. "*Wonder how she manages on a boat in this outfit. Maybe this is her selling outfit, not her sailing outfit.*"

Walking down the dock, Mary put her hand on Jeff's arm. Jeff looked over at her, his eyes looked down at her cleavage. Mary smiled, inhaled, and the third button sprang free.

"Oh Dear!" she squeaked, stepping in front of Jeff. Facing him, not with her back to him for modesty, but with her back towards her boyfriend. She took a long time getting everything back in the shirt, and even longer trying to get the button fastened. Jeff just watched. He was fantasizing what it would be like to sail away for a week, or a month, or…with a woman like this on a boat with a cabin.

He snapped out of his revelry as they approached the boat. The paint was old and flakey. Well, it could be repainted. Jeff wondered when the photo of the boat had been taken. The sail stuffed around the spars looked very old, wrinkled, and dirty; even worse, the boom and gaff were swinging from the end of a halyard.

A scruffy-looking man called out, "Welcome aboard. Name's Bob."

"Thanks," said Jeff. "Looking forward to—"

"His boat is really beautiful," said Mary. "What kinda boat—"

"Maybe we could work out a trade, you know," said Bob, taking Jeff's hand and guiding him to a seat in the rear of the cockpit. Mary sat on a little step in front of the closed wooden hatch, blocking access to the cabin.

"Why are you selling your boat?" asked Jeff, looking around, noticing some old paint cans on the forward deck. A large pile of junk sat on the dock, next to the boat.

Bob looked at Mary.

"We want a bigger boat," she said. "We want to sail down the coast to Mexico and then …the world."

Jeff moved forward to investigate the cabin, Mary didn't move aside, just flashed a big smile at him.

"We got a new, sail-away price today," said Bob, jumping up and standing in front of Jeff. "Your boat plus a thousand, and she's yours today."

"I want to see below."

"Oh, hell. I'll take nine hundred."

Jeff moved to the hatch. Mary's smile faded as she scooted aside. The wooden rails were swollen tight. Pushing hard, the hatch slid open. Jeff was greeted and engulfed by the stench of mildew. The electric bilge pump kicked on. A sucking, slurping sound filled the space. Even in the low light, Jeff could see dirty, oily bilge water sloshing around.

"Great potential," said Bob. "You could build in anything. She's built on a lifeboat hull. Very seaworthy."

"What kind of engine is that?" Jeff asked, looking down.

"An air-cooled Onan, from an electric generator. No cooling water intake. The exhaust goes through the roof. No through hull fittings."

And no inside stove or heater either, Jeff thought as he descended into the space. It did have potential, but did he really want another project? He touched the engine. It was still warm.

"How do you start this thing?"

Bob reached in and hit a switch. The engine turned over very slowly, arrrrru, arrrrru, arrru, but did not fire.

"Must be cold, haven't run it for a while," said Bob, stepping in through the hatch with one foot on the flywheel. He pressed the starter switch and kicked the large wheel to help spin the engine. It started.

"Works every time," Bob said with a grin.

"Turn it off! It's too loud!" shouted Jeff, emerging up into the cockpit. Without looking at either Bob or Mary, he stepped onto the dock.

Bob kept up a patter of questions and comments but elicited no response from the potential buyer.

Walking forward, then back amidships, Jeff knelt beside the chain plates that connected the rigging from the mast down to the side of the hull. He pushed the boat out about a foot or so from the dock. The water was clear, even here in the city's harbor, the bottom was visible. A crab scurried past. Sunlight illuminated the water on the other side of the boat. The hull was clearly visible. Straps from the chain plates angled down underwater to support a stack of steel construction I-beams forming a keel.

Jeff felt his body turning numb. He had never seen such a total violation of nautical design, safety, and engineering. The boat assumed another appearance. It was ugly, very ugly.

Jeff stood, and without looking back, walked up the dock towards his beloved, beautiful boat.

Mary ran and caught up. She chattered nonstop. A few paces from the boat, Mary grabbed his arm. He glanced over, noticing her breasts jiggling as she ran. He pulled away, disgusted. Disgusted with himself for allowing his fantasy of owning a larger cruising boat with a bunk, and yes, having a woman in that bed, to almost blank out his common sense. Why had he not asked more questions about the boat?

Jeff freed his mooring lines, shoved his boat away from the dock, and started his engine.

Lunch at a small cafe in the harbor took longer than expected. Their private dock was crowded, and it took a while for him to tie up.

His hamburger and fries got cold as Jeff sat staring out over the harbor. He knew that he was vulnerable, wanting a woman, or more honestly, a loving relationship. A boat with a cabin was one way. Thinking of Mary made him angry, he did not like his hormones manipulated. The ferry came and left. He thought he saw the "dream boat" leaving the area almost hidden by the departing ferry. About an hour later the next ferry arrived. It was getting late. Jeff finished his lunch and returned to his boat. He enjoyed the challenge of sailing without using the engine. It took some maneuvering and time to clear the Winslow harbor and head out to Puget Sound.

About half an hour into the crossing, the wind died. His boat sailed well in light winds, but now he could barely make steerage way. Jeff kept sailing, making slow headway. He did not want to start the engine, there was always hope the wind would pick up. It was hard to tell if he was making progress, maybe the slow movement through the water was just movement against the tide. He had checked the tide table before his morning departure, but now the crossing was much later. The tide was going to be very low when he arrived at the locks. Maybe the currents in the Sound were different with this approaching ebb tide. It was almost dark.

He started the small outboard engine and turned on his running lights.

Arriving at the locks the traffic light was green for the small lock. Jeff was relieved, it had been a long day. As he approached, he wondered if at low tide the lock master could even see the top of his mast above the lock walls.

"Hey Eric, you're right. There is a boat down there."

THEIR

I'm hungry, at least that's what I think the ache in the pit of my stomach is telling me. I can't face eating another greasy, shopping center pizza in front of my TV. Driving past a mall, I spot an Indian restaurant. I ate there a couple of months ago and it was pretty good. A real mom 'n pop place, considering the staff, maybe even a brother/sister place.

"Welcome," says the young person at the door, "Nice to see you again."

As I'm being seated, I wonder if they really remember me or if that's just their friendly greeting. I ask them for a plate of papadam to start. Looking over the top of my menu, I see another person coming in. They are seated at the next table, very close to me. Our eyes meet, just a glance, a quick smile. We both look away.

I know what I want to order and put my menu down. My garbanzo bean crisps arrive. I feel awkward eating, acutely aware of my very close neighbor trying to select from the menu. They have short hair with flecks of gray and are dressed in stylish clothes.

"Have you eaten here before?" They ask. "Any suggestions?"

"Yes, the food here is very good," I say. "If you like Indian food." I pass over the appetizer plate. "Here, have some chips while you decide."

Together, we consult the menu.

"Do you like lamb?" I ask.

"Yes. Medium spicy."

"Great. Do you like mushrooms?" again, I ask.

"Yes."

"Do you like okra?"

"No," they say.

"Do you like eggplant?"

"Yes.

"Do you like daal, you know lentil soup?"

"Yes."

"I wonder if they have goat?" I ask with a grin.

"I'll pass on that."

We laugh and put down our menus.

"You know," I say, "everything you've selected is what I would order." I explain that each of these servings is enough for two. It's too much food unless you want to eat take-home for days.

"I know it may sound strange, but…you know…maybe we could just share our order. It's really okay if you don't—"

"Sounds good to me."

They move over to my table and continue eating my papadam.

"Can you see the waiter?" I say. "They should be here soon to take our requests."

We place our order, including okra, some bread, and add a good bottle of California Pinot. Conversation is easy, much to my relief. I have missed being with, and talking with, an interesting person. Our subjects range from the weather to the economy and even venture into politics. Fortunately, we're on the same page.

The subject of grandchildren enters our conversation. As we brag about our off-spring, I mention that I have a trans grandchild.

"Not really a child, they are twenty-two."

"How are you doing with that?" asks my table mate.

"It's been a challenge, and a learning," I answer. "They want me to use the gender-neutral pronoun 'they' because everyone's at a different place on the gender spectrum. I've been trying."

"Yes, I've noticed you have—"

"It's hard. I've been looking at other people for so long in binary categories, through a screen of socially accepted sexual values. You know; man/woman, broad shoulders, big breasts…" I stop and glance across the table, worried I've offended.

We both laugh nervously.

We eat in silence, searching for an easier topic.

"Do you have any plans for a vacation?" they ask, "You know, a cruise or something?"

I look down at the feast before me. My chin starts to quiver. The earlier pain in my stomach returns. I try not to cry. My breathing is shallow and difficult.

"What…?" they ask.

I explain. "Three years ago, my spouse and I made plans to take a cruise in Europe. The first step was getting physicals so we could start off in a good place. That's when, uh when…" I'm choking up.

They sit quietly watching me.

"We found that—" I swallow and continue. "The 'Big C' had joined us. Our life became focused on the cancer. It grew very fast." I sip water trying to dislodge the lump in my throat. "The day we were to set sail, my mate took a different trip, across—" I can no longer hold the tears back. "They crossed over." I take a deep breath. "That was a year ago today."

"I'm sorry," comes a soft voice from across the table. "I lost my partner about three years ago."

I feel genuine comfort, but I also wonder if the word "partner" is telling me that their relationship was 'same sex.' I hear my grand-child shouting in my ear, "There you go again, putting your old evaluations on people."

We continue eating in silence.

When we finish, the waiter comes, boxes up the remaining food, and leaves the check. Before I can make a move, my dinner companion lays a credit card on the table.

"I get all the leftovers," they say, "including the okra, which I loved."

Neither of us is in a hurry to leave, and there's a little wine left.

We finished the wine. I realize I don't want this to be our last meal together.

"I, um, I'd like to see you again," I say, feeling my face flush, and not just from the wine.

"Me too," they say. "Hand me your phone and I'll put in my number." Their eyes look very shiny as I slide over my phone.

"Give me yours too, please...Umm. I'm not familiar with this make," I say. "How do I enter my phone number?"

"Easy..."

They reach over. Our hands touch. It feels natural.

I enter my name, 'Morgan' and my number.

They return my phone. I can see their contact information: 'Lee' with a local number.

Our hands are inches apart. We touch.

The touch becomes a holding. Fingers laced together. It feels good.

I look into Lee's eyes. Their face changes, morphs into a wrinkled old, gray-haired person with bright twinkling eyes. Is this an assurance, a certainty from the future?

We smile.

MAXINE

I saw her standing on the church steps as I made the turn for my last lap. Mowing the church lawn was part of my job as janitor. It was hot, muggy hot as only southern Illinois can be. My white T shirt was draped over the mower's handlebar. She was dressed, as usual, in black as if she was going to a funeral.

"Hi Charlie."

"Hi Maxine," I said, bending over to turn off the mower.

She stepped closer. "Sure is hot today."

"Yep."

"I brought over some ice tea." She handed me a large glass, the ice cubes clinking with a refreshing chime.

"Do you want to sit on the steps in the shade?"

"Oh geez, thanks, this is the best!"

I tried to keep from draining the glass in one long gulp. Raising the glass for a second sip, a bead of sweat rolled down my bare chest. Maxine was staring at me, down at my body. I had forgotten to slip on my shirt. The white band of my briefs showed above my low riding jeans. Was it the same for a woman, as with us men, the excitement of seeing a flash of white undies? I began to feel a little self-conscious.

"Charlie, could you help me for a minute? I need to get a bag of mulch for the garden out of my car?"

"Of course," I answered. She lived just across the street from the church.

Maxine opened the car trunk. The bag of mulch took up much of the space

"Do you want me to bring around the wheelbarrow?"

"Nah, I got it."

She stood very close to me as I reached down to pick up the bag. It was heavier than I thought and my hand slipped off, my elbow hit her in the chest.

"Oh, I'm so sorry. I'm …My hand slipped…"

"It's okay," she said, rubbing her breast.

"You sure you're okay?" I said, watching her touching herself. I threw the T shirt over my shoulder, and hoisted the bag up. It was easy for me to carry the large bag to her garden.

"Oh thank you so much. How can I repay you?"

With an exaggerated movement, I swept off my hat and bowed.

"It's a pleasure being of service," I said with a phony southern drawl.

We both laughed.

She touched my sweaty arm for a long moment. A flash of energy shot through my whole body and paused too long for comfort in my groin. Glancing down, I couldn't help but notice the top button of her blouse was open. I could see the thin white line of her bra top.

"I gotta go," I said and dashed back to the church.

Locking the church door behind me, I went to the restroom to take care of the painful bulge in my jeans.

The next Saturday, Maxine was not around while I mowed the church lawn. It was a toss-up between relief and disappointment, but I admit I had hoped to see her. But why? I asked myself. She's an old woman. Not really old, just older than me. She always dressed in black and wore her hair up in an old lady style. But when she stood close to me, she smelled like, like…something fresh, a young fresh. Her smile was warm and inviting, or was I fantasizing?

I was 18 (well, I would be next month), was over six-feet tall, wore cowboy boots, and had a hard body from my summer work. A mustache had grown over the summer. At the first day of school assembly, the principal welcomed all 126 of us back, but added that Charles's new facial hair was not welcome. He said it with a laugh and the whole school joined in. I smiled and gave him a thumbs-up. We were also not allowed to turn our shirt collars up in a rebellious statement. I shaved the next morning before school.

The weather changed and I didn't have to mow the church lawn. But with the fall chill in the air, the church's two big coal furnaces had to be fired up. The furnaces were lit Saturday evening after my supper, and for two hours I cleaned and dusted the church. The fires had to be checked every twenty minutes to make sure they were burning correctly.

I accepted spending my Saturday evenings doing my job. I would have rather been on a date, but my attempts at this were failures. All the girls in school were looking for a husband to be snatched up and corralled upon graduation. The industrial arts shop class even had a senior project to build a cedar chest for your girlfriend, storage for a young couple's wool blankets protected from moths.

After completing my cleaning jobs, but still waiting on the furnace fires, I turned off all but one small light in the large sanctuary. The church proudly owned a magnificent pipe organ. I climbed on the high organ seat and played. I had taken some piano lessons, so knew a few simple tunes. The most fun was playing and experimenting with the organ stops. I discovered what "all stops" really meant, bringing all the organ pipes to play at the same time.

The organ had a volume peddle. Laying my hand flat on the keys, fingertips sounding the highest notes, rolling my arm down, playing and holding every note, increasing the volume with my foot, the resulting sound was unearthly. I laughed out loud like a mad man. With only one small bulb lit in the cavernous sanctuary, it even frightened me for a moment.

"That was really scary," came a voice out of the darkness.

"Who's there?

"Just me Charlie, Maxine."

I turned and saw a small, dark figure drifting down the aisle towards the organ. Maxine settled herself on the organ seat next to me. I was so embarrassed. I tried to say something, but nothing came out.

"That looks like fun," she said with a grin, "I've always wanted to play the organ, but was too afraid to even ask. You are either incredibly brave or incredibly—"

"Stupid," I interrupt.

"Well, that's not what I was going to say, but close enough." She laughed.

We sat there for a while, playing a few notes and pulling stops in and out. She was too short to reach the pedals.

"Do you know Chop Sticks?" she asked, "Four hands?"

Maxine slid closer, placed one arm over mine, and started to play. I joined in. Our hands were spread across the whole keyboard. With my longer arms, the upper keyboard was within reach, and with it a whole new selection of stops. However, working the foot pedals was a disaster. We laughed so hard we couldn't continue playing.

"I've never had so much fun, and in this old church too."

"Yeah, I know what you mean. How did you get in? I thought I had locked the doors."

"You did, I have a key," she said. "But that's a long story. You know, my grandpa gave this organ to the church."

Maxine swung around on the seat, facing me. There was just enough light to see her face. She related how her grandpa had given the organ in thanks for the safe return of his son from WWI. His son was her father.

"Wow!" I said. "That's wonderful."

"Yes, *he* came back alive. It's…wonderful."

The sound of the last syllable came out as a little chirp.

Maxine buried her face in my shoulder. I slid my arm out from between us and held her. I could not hear her crying but felt her body shuttering from sobs deep inside of her. I had never had a woman cry in my arms. This wasn't fantasy. This was closeness, intimacy, sharing. I shifted in my seat and held her closer. A swirl of something wrapped around us. Was it light, or colors, or sounds? My heart gave a powerful thump just where she rested her cheek. This was love.

I admit it turned me on. But what do I do next? Love with and for a woman was very new to me.

Maxine looked up at me. Even in the low light, I could see that her face was wet with tears.

"What?" I asked.

"Shhh, I'll tell you later."

She said she had to return home before her mother started to worry about where she was. The big church door thudded shut, the lock clicking into place. This whole evening had been great, just great, but it left me confused. Fantasies started filling my mind. These I could handle. It was reality I was having difficulty with.

The path across the town park was the shortest way home, but going up Main Street offered a glimpse of Maxine through the window at her desk. She and her brother had an insurance office on Main at First. Every day, after band practice at school, I rode my bike past hoping to get a glimpse and a smile, or even a wave from her.

One day, three guys were standing in front of her window. I was not going fast. The biggest guy stepped off the curb and grabbed one side of my handlebars. My fall turned into a roll, and I recovered on my feet. Walking quickly, up the curb, I faced the three toughs who had backed up to Maxine's window. Our fists were clenched, at the ready, just above the belt. We might have been Bantam roosters strutting before a fight. There was a smirk on the leader's face. He was ready for any kind of verbal confrontation. My right arm shot straight out at his nose. My fist made contact with a loud, sickening pop. Pulling my right fist back gave added energy to my left arm. The fist came up under his chin, snapping his head back against her window with a very loud bang. The window glass did not break, but I saw her jump back out of danger.

The leader fell forward on his knees; blood, lots of blood gushing from his nose.

"You broke my nose!" he moaned.

"Yeah, and there's a lot more I'll break," I responded. "If you ever touch me or my bike again, I'll hit you so hard you'll have to open your mouth to take a shit."

I had always wanted to use that threat ever since I learned it in grade school, but never had the opportunity. The three left, the leader holding his broken nose, his shirt front soaked in blood.

Maxine came out and asked if I was okay. She saw my right hand was bloody. "You better come in and let me take a look at it."

I followed her into the restroom. She examined each finger, gently holding my hand under cold running water. It hurt.

"None are broken, but you do have an open wound," she said. "You know, you can't hit someone like they do in the movies without hurting yourself."

She bandaged the cut. I was sitting, and as she bent over my hand, I could not help but see that the top two buttons of her blouse were open. I stared. She looked up and saw where my eyes were focused, and smiled, but didn't close the buttons.

We had a cold snap in the coming weeks. One Saturday afternoon, a light rain froze and made the streets very slippery. I didn't want to ride my bike to the church. I told my folks I might be home late; I needed to make sure the furnaces were working so the church would be warm on Sunday morning. I didn't tell them I was hoping Maxine would come over while I was working.

Lights from inside illuminated the stained glass windows as I approached the church. The door was locked, but when I went in Maxine was dusting the communion table in front of the church just below the pulpit.

"Hi," I greeted her. "Thanks for the help. Do you want to play the organ again?"

"No, not tonight. I thought you might come over after your chores and have some tea. Mother is away visiting her sister, so we don't have to be quiet."

"Sounds good to me."

"I made some chocolate chip cookies…"

"My favorite!"

"I'll stick around until you're through."

"Won't take long. I have one furnace running. I fired it up when the cold snap hit. You know, keep the pipes from freezing. The other starts easily."

I turned off the lights and made sure the door was locked.

The front steps of the church were very slippery. I hoped I would remember to sprinkle sand on Sunday morning.

"Be careful," I said, taking Maxine's hand. At the bottom of the slippery steps, she didn't let go. Did I imagine it, or was she holding on tighter? We held hands crossing the narrow street to her home.

Together we entered the small parlor, just off the large, formal living room. It was cozy. A fireplace with a small coal fire heated the room. I took off my warm coat. Maxine returned with a tray of tea and cookies. She took off her coat. Underneath she wore a very thin white blouse which easily revealed her bra and her beautiful curves.

There were two chairs on either side of a small window and a couch facing the chairs and the window. She sat on the couch, taking one of the two spaces. Patting the area beside her, she smiled up at me. I tried not to look at her breasts. They were so very beautiful. Maxine poured the tea. I focused on the couch, it was very old. There was a lot of dark, ornately carved wood. The upholstery was woven horsehair. The smooth, dark surface was a joy to touch. It seemed alive. I ran my fingers again and again over the surface.

"Feels good, doesn't it?" said Maxine, "This house and all the furnishings were my grandparents. I love to touch it. And I thought you might like it too."

"I do, I learn a lot by touching." I thought about touching her breasts. This room, this intimacy was making my head spin. What should I do? Was she inviting me or teasing me? Looking out the window, most of the view was blocked by a boxwood hedge. Across the small street, the front of the tall church loomed towards me. It was dark, even in the moonlight, the stained glass windows shiny black, no light from inside to brighten the colored glass. The stories, so beautifully crafted in glass remained dark. Divine stories of love and forgiveness remained unseen. Only the lighter gothic stone that framed the glass was prominent. It looked like praying hands. Were they trying to say something to me?

Maxine served me a cup of tea and said to help myself to her… what did she say? She must have said cookies. I glanced back at the looming, praying hands.

We chatted for a bit. I couldn't concentrate on what she said.

"This is really a beautiful house," I said, "It's fortunate that your grandpa's son came back from the war, and you are here."

"Yes, fortunate, god-damn fortunate!" she shouted. "He was given a life…" Maxine tore her little tea napkin into shreds. I put out my hand and lightly held her fists. She pulled my hand up to her breast and held it there. It was so very soft, more so than I had ever fantasized. It was not 'a couple of melons' as some guys talked about. Her breasts were alive, pulsating with energy. The vibrations speeding through my body transforming me into… into a man desiring this woman.

"Oh, Charlie hold me."

So I did, wondering what to do next. I had never been this close to a woman. I glanced out the window. The church was looming very large. Was it saying something about premarital sex?

"I loved him! You are so much like him, even your soft curls." She reached up and ran her fingers through my hair. It felt nice, her touching me. "His name was also Charlie."

"We were planning to get married right after graduation. He was eighteen and I would have been by the spring." She looked down, rubbing her ring finger. "He loved airplanes and was trying to decide whether to go to college and study aeronautical engineering or join his father running their sizable farm. Because of the damn war, the colleges shut down their engineering programs. He enlisted, as did a lot of guys in the senior class."

"The Air Force needed him, so he left before graduation.

"He…never came back." She was crying again. "His plane was 'missing in action' but there was hope. Always hope. For years I've had hope. I knew he was gone but held unto that hope for fourteen years." She lifted her head, "I never thought I could love another man."

She moved around and wrapped both arms around me, pressing her body into mine.

"Until you came into my life," she said, "I love you Charlie, thanks for awakening my buried passion."

I gathered my courage and said, "I want to make love with you."

"I know. I can feel it in you. It's nice to be desired. I guess I'm not so old as I thought. I may not be eighteen, but thirty-two isn't so bad."

"I've never been with a woman," I said, "Will you teach me?"

"Oh Charlie, Charlie, I don't know that much. I've had sex only once, the night before my Charlie left. Then for years I have carried the guilt of premarital sex with me. I knew it was okay; we were engaged. I had the church key. We stood before the altar and recited the 'Do you?' questions. Charlie pronounced us married and kissed the bride. The kiss continued and we ended down on the floor." Maxine glanced out the window. "We had sex. Over the years, the memory became a fantasy. But it also carried guilt."

"Yeah, I know what you mean. I think that's also been a large part of my life," I said. "Even now, I feel the church is looking down at us in judgment."

Maxine slid off my lap and closed the drapes. She coughed, the curtains had not been adjusted for many years. We both sneezed from the dust. Someone once said that an orgasm was like a sneeze. I hoped not.

Recovering from our mutual sneeze, Maxine added another lump of coal to the fire. There was a smell of sulfur in the air as the new lump caught.

"If I were, and I'm not, superstitious, I would say that I smell Lucifer, the Devil here," I said with a grin. "Maybe he's here tempting us to…"

"Oh Charlie, you are…"

"Right now, I would take my chance. I don't think it's the Devil. I think it's love."

Maxine came to me, embracing and kissing me. I slid my hands down to her hips and …

"No," she whispered. "I can't. I want to but I just can't."

She didn't release her embrace, still pressing against me. She must have felt the bulge in my jeans.

I didn't know what to do. I'd never been in this kind of situation. I started to move. She stepped back but continued holding my hands.

"Go now," she said. "Before I change my mind. You have to check the fires in the church."

I was so hot, I had forgotten. Running across the street, slamming the church door behind me, I heard the latch click and lock. I ran down the aisle to the furnaces. I made it as far as the communion table. It was like an altar. Leaning back against its strength, I spilled my seed on the ground. Just like it said not to in the Old Testament Scripture.

The next day, Sunday, Maxine was not in attendance. This concerned me. Was she okay? I stayed after church service to shut down the furnaces and pick up any trash in the pews. Hymnals left on the seats had to be returned to their racks on the pew back. I was near the front of the church when I heard the big door thud shut and the lock click in.

Maxine was walking down the aisle, barely recognizable. She looked very light, a big smile on her face. The smile seemed to take in her whole body. Her hair was down and she wasn't wearing black, I had never seen her in public this way.

"Hi, I want to show you something," she said, leaning back on the table next to me. Her radiance seemed to fill the whole sanctuary. Here she was, in the front of the church, where we played the organ, where she and her Charlie got married and consummated the union on the floor. The very floor, where last night, I...

"Last night, after you left," Maxine said, "I pulled out all my old letters. The few Charlie had written, and the many of mine that had been returned. I burned the whole collection in the parlor fireplace."

She pulled out an old postcard tucked in her blouse. She was beaming. It was a photo, in old color, of a ship sailing out underneath a beautiful, rust-red bridge. Under the picture was written: Golden Gate Bridge, San Francisco, California. She read the message on the back.

Leaving tomorrow, sailing out under this red bridge. Love Charlie

"I have looked and reread this card hundreds of times."

Maxine smiled at me through her tears.

"These were the last words from him. For years I have tried to follow his directive: Love Charlie. He sailed out under this bridge and never came back. He is gone."

Ripping the card into four pieces, she said, "I want to burn this in the church furnace."

The fire in the big furnace was still burning hot. With its door open, I rested a long, steel-handled shovel on the shelf. Maxine placed the four postcard scraps on the shovel and added the old brass church key.

"You burn it," she said, "In the hottest part of the flame. I want to be rid of it." We watched. It was gone in a flash of yellow white fire.

We returned to the sanctuary and side-by-side leaned back against the solid altar table.

"I want to thank you for helping me."

"How so?" I asked.

"You helped me see that I'm a woman and can be desired by a man. That I can love a man and enjoy his touch."

"That's for sure," I said.

"I'm going to San Francisco. I've never been there. If I like it, I'm moving there. I'm having Sunday dinner today with my brother, I'm going to tell him."

"That's wonderful," I said. "San Francisco has to be a great place to live. I'm looking forward to getting away from here too." I reached over and placed my hand on hers. She moved closer.

"I've always seen you as a loving and lovable woman," I said. "I'm so happy that you see it too. You have helped me to see what qualities I want in a woman. And if I have to wait until I'm thirty-two, then I will."

Maxine poked me in the ribs.

"Oh, you're mean." She laughed, "I'm not too old, you are too young!"

We stood for a while in silence, leaning against the table.

"Why," I ask. "Did you burn up the old church key?"

I could see she was trying to find the right words.

"Ah, well, to be perfectly honest, sometimes I would come over to the church, lay down here where my Charlie and I made love, and well, you know, fantasize. That's over."

"And now you can fantasize about me. I wish we had made love, and…"

"No," Maxine said, backing away, "Eventually you would leave, and that is too painful."

I leaned over and whispered in her ear.

"I fantasize about you," I said, "Sometimes I—"

"I know you do."

A few days later, I walked my bike past Maxine's office window. There was an empty space where her desk had been.

Maxine was gone.

A KANSAS SUMMER STORM

Buddy turned off the engine of the old '36 Chevy truck. His uncle and cousin were harvesting the far end of the field, their two combines cutting swaths through the ripe wheat. It would be a while before he needed to sidle up to them, fill up the truck, and drive another load to the grain elevator in town. He loved this old Chevy; it was older than he was. He was fifteen, well, he would be in a month. Buddy liked driving the truck alongside the moving combines, adjusting his position and speed until he was exactly under the offload spout to receive the new crop of wheat.

A few minutes later, his cousin David brought the gigantic combine around, but instead of allowing Buddy to position the truck alongside for off-loading, he stopped. Disappointed, Buddy jumped out and climbed up into the combine's noisy cab.

David pointed to the sky. "Have you seen that black, anvil-shaped cloud coming in from the North?" He had to shout to be heard over the roar of the combine. "We're in for some heavy weather, rain for sure, maybe a tornado."

"Yeah," Buddy said. "What about those angry, dark clouds forming up in the South?"

David looked over his shoulder. "Oh, damn! Is that…? Did I just see a funnel shape drop out of those clouds?" Continuing to shout, he explained that tornados generally traveled north from southwest to northeast. And since that funnel was directly south, it should move and pass to the east of them.

"However," he said, "keep an eye on it. I'm going to work at this end of the field so I can easily get out when the rain starts. Why don't you go on down to the far end and off-load the other machine."

The wind had shifted by the time Buddy reached the end. It was so cold, he shivered. The wind brought the smell of first rain on dry soil. Buddy inhaled deeply; he loved the distinct, rich smell. He wondered if there was a name for it.

A few large drops of rain fell. The dark cloud completely blocked out the sun.

Uncle Hugh pulled up and jumped out of the second combine. The wind blew off his favorite cap. He stopped, looked back at his cap blowing away, and came to Buddy's window. "Rain's coming. You take the truck through the break in the fence and back along the path in the pasture."

"It's getting dark," Buddy yelled over the combine's engine. "And I don't know where the break is. How do I get into the pasture?"

"Get out," Hugh shouted. "I'll take the truck. You take the combine back."

FLASH!

Everything lit up. The huge combine, silhouetted against the sky, stood very big on the flat prairie. In that brief moment, it appeared monstrous, and overpowering.

Buddy counted: one…two…three…four…five…sixBOOM!

The rain was coming down harder. It was almost dark. Buddy could barely make out Hugh and the old truck. The headlights came on, bringing a smile to Buddy's face. He had wanted to see those headlights, those beautiful old torpedo-shaped lights mounted on top of the fenders, shining at night.

FLASH!   one…two…three…four…fiveBOOM   RUMBLE rumble

"Five miles," Buddy said. "Getting closer. He climbed the steps into the combine's cab. He sat still for a moment, feeling the engine rumbling. This was only his second time sitting in the operator's seat. His cousin had explained all the controls: the throttle speed lever: slow, medium, and fast, the larger lever that adjusted the belts on the variable speed drive pulleys, left and right brake pedals, and all the others needed to adjust harvesting machinery.

FLASH! one…two…three…fourBOOM

"Four miles, getting closer."

Buddy eased forward. It was like maneuvering a small house. The rain was coming down harder. Ahead, to the west, a small patch of bright sky appeared beyond the dark cloud overhead.

FLASH!……..BOOM

He forgot to count. Buddy steered towards the glimpse of sky. It was very dark, hard to see. He turned on the powerful head lights. The falling rain reflected back silver-white streaks, blinding his vision. He turned the lights off. A new sound rose above the roar of the engine, a loud din from the metal body of the combine being pummeled.

"That's more than rain, it's hail."

FLASH! one…twoBAMMMMM rumble rumble!

"Two miles. How much closer?"

The momentary flash lit marble-sized hail bouncing off the machine.

"Geez, that would hurt!"

The combine's tractor-size tires started to slip. The rain had made the field muddy and slippery. The left tire spun, digging down through the soil looking for traction. As the combine surged forward, the right tire began to spin and dig, throwing the machine off course. Buddy turned the steering wheel to correct his direction. Nothing happened. The smaller wheels in the back, used for steering, slipped sideways in the slick mud, no traction.

FLASH! oneBOOOOM!

The clap of thunder, so close, left a ringing in Buddy's ears. The brief flash of lightning illuminated a pond, a puddle, maybe a small lake directly in his path. He steered away from the standing water using the left or right wheel brakes.

Another flash revealed the end of the field and the road beyond. He didn't see the funnel cloud and wondered where it was. The belt drive (as opposed to chain or solid shaft drive) was slipping. It wasn't engineered to operate in rainy, wet conditions. Buddy pushed the forward speed control all the way. The combine continued to move forward accompanied by a high-pitched scream from the tortured belt drive.

FLASHBOOOM!

"Less than a mile away," Buddy said. "It must have struck the metal corner stake of the field a half mile away. I'm the tallest object in the field. Am I next?"

He knew there was nothing he could do, just keep going.

The rain let up; the hail stopped. Buddy switched on the headlights. In the feeble light, he could just make out the end of the field. A lone figure stood there, barely perceptible. Moving closer, he saw it was David's sister, his cousin Janis, wearing a yellow slicker, shiny wet in his headlights. She pointed the beam of her flashlight at the open gate between the field and the road.

Buddy waved a thank you, bounced through a shallow ditch, and up onto the road. He was going too fast. The ditch on the far side of the road was too deep to drive across. In the space of one second, in the distance traveled of five feet, he pulled the speed control lever back, turned the steering wheel to the left, and stomped as hard as he could on the left brake pedal.

The huge machine pivoted on the left wheel, the tire gouging a deep divot on the road surface. Buddy lifted his foot, straightened the steering wheel, and set the speed control on low. He glanced back over his shoulder,

FLASH! One...BOOM!

One mile away. The lightning strike probably hit an old, worn-out, rusty combine discarded in the pasture beyond.

Janis stood with her back to Buddy. No one had seen his graceful, ballet-like turn in the road. But he knew. He felt pride.

He drove on, crossing the bridge over the deep ditch on the right, heading to the large, metal barn behind the house. David was standing in the open, twelve-foot-wide doors. Buddy swung the combine around and stopped parallel to the doors. He did not want to attempt the tricky maneuver of driving an eighteen-foot-wide machine through a twelve-foot door.

David took over, tweaking the combine through the door, and into the spacious barn.

"Wow!" he said. "The drive belts are really slipping. I'm surprised you made it back. Good work."

Buddy was grinning, and shivering. David picked up an old coat someone had tossed on the workbench, shook out the dust and handed it to him.

Looking out the door, David said, "Here comes Hugh and the truck. Wonder what took him so long."

Hugh backed the loaded truck into the barn and stopped in the space left between the two combines. He shouted, "Open the tailgate!"

With the back open, and the hydraulic system slowly lifting the truck bed, Hugh inched forward dumping the wheat on the concrete floor. David and Buddy picked up scoop shovels and spread out the crop to dry. They made fast work of it. In fifteen minutes, the harvest was saved.

Buddy was no longer shivering; the work had warmed him. He stood between Hugh and David in the open door watching it rain. No one spoke.

The clouds were moving away, light was returning.

"Well," said Hugh. "With this rain and hail, harvest's over. The fields are too muddy. I'm surprised you made it back. I almost got stuck in the pasture. The old buffalo wallow had already filled with water."

"Yep," said Buddy. "I thought I was going to get bogged down in that low place in the field."

Hugh returned Buddy's look, they were the same height, six feet. Their eyes locked for a moment. Buddy felt the connection. It was good. Hugh's face was stark white from the top of his ears to his receding hairline where his lost cap had protected it from the sun. Below his clenched jaw, the lower part of his face and the "V" on his chest from an open shirt were deep mahogany red-brown, burned from long hours working in the sun above the high prairie of western Kansas. With their eyes locked, Buddy could sense what Hugh was seeing from this summer storm. Eyes that had seen hail, tornados, droughts, and much more.

Now, as before, the only way through was to just keep going.

Hugh reached up to push his cap back and realized it was gone. "Guess I'll get a new cap, maybe a green one. That'll be a John Deere Tractor cap. Never had one before."

"But Dad," David said. "We don't even own a piece of John Deere equipment."

"I know," Hugh said. "But I like the color."

They stood together in silence. Each with his own thoughts.

David stood over six-foot-two in his cowboy work boots. "You know, we got most of the harvest done. Only a little left in this last field. We got plenty of wheat for seed next year." David turned and smiled at Buddy. "And I think we have a man to operate the combine next summer. Hey, Bud. You comin' back?"

"You betcha!" said Bud.

David reached out and gave Bud a hug. Hugh put a hand on Bud's shoulder. Bud grinned, feeling the warmth.

Three men stood in the open door, looking at the sky.

FOUND IT

Six or seven boys, on their knees, dug expectantly into a dirt bank behind their school, looking for .50 caliber machine gun bullets. Above the excited schoolboys, leaned a rusty Japanese gun emplacement. A remnant from when Japan attacked Manila only a few hours after Pearl Harbor and occupied the Philippine Islands during WWII. There had been a firefight here in the schoolyard; now it was a good place to find old ammunition.

Will stood behind them, watching his 6th-grade classmates. He did not want to get dirty during school recess. They all were dressed in the style of foreign (American and European) business-men: white cotton shorts with a cuff just above the knees, white socks just below the knees, and a loose shirt. Will was a year older than the other boys but was much smaller, a good head shorter. He had suffered from malnutrition as a young boy living in the concentration camps set up by the occupying Japanese forces.

"I found it!" shouted one of the diggers. "I found one, I knew it was here."

Everyone, including Will, crowded around to see.

"Is it a tracer?" asked Will, who was usually quiet, speaking only when addressed.

The boy turned the bullet around to check the back, no hole.

"Oh, guess not, too bad."

All the boys had collections of old bullets from WW II. At this time, in the 1950s, they seemed to be everywhere if one looked. The tracer shell was prized. One shell in five, fired from a machine gun, its pyrotechnic illumination helped the gunner to see where his shots were aimed. On the front wall of their school, an arc of bullet holes pockmarked the concrete surface. Every fifth hole was stained from the fiery heat of a tracer shell. The line of the machine gun spray crossed a window. Will wondered if there had been a person standing there when the gun blasted the opening. He felt a grab deep in his stomach.

The school bell rang, the boys shuffled back to class. Will followed behind, looking like a little brother tagging along.

School let out for the day about 1:00 pm. Like most of the students, Will was picked up by his family's driver and car. He saw his friend Charlie struggling to carry a backpack stuffed with homework books. No one ever picked him up.

"Hey, do you want a ride?"

"That would be great, thanks!"

Will helped lift the book bag into the back seat, giving out a loud grunt. "God, this is heavy!"

"Yeah, a lot more homework in the 7th grade."

"All the more reason to look forward to next year," Will said, with a shrug. They were a grade apart, but the same age.

When they reached Charlie's home, he asked Will if he would like to come in for lunch. Will paused for a long time, then explained that his mother was home today, and he should go home.

"But maybe I could…Yes, definitely! Someday."

Charlie's parents were American college professors who helped to restore war-damaged schools. They didn't fit into the wealthy, foreign business world, or the US military presence.

Whenever Will knew his mother would not be home, he invited Charlie for lunch. Will was afraid of his mother. She was often angry, yelling at him and the household staff. The kitchen maid and the cook made delicious Filipino food. Chicken adobo with vinegar, soy sauce, and noodles was his favorite. Will's father, also an American, was in the business community, but he was rarely at home. He devoted his time to rebuilding his coconut oil company; it had been destroyed during the war.

The boys spent afternoons laughing and playing and talking boy talk. Charlie never saw Will's father smile the few times they met. No wonder Will rarely spoke out at school. The first time they played in Will's pool, Charlie asked Will why he had not gone swimming with the rest of the guests at a fellow student's birthday party, a few weeks before.

"Haven't you noticed?" replied Will. "I can't swim. I have to use a paddleboard. My chest is caved in, and my legs are crooked. I don't want to be made fun of."

"I never thought about it," said Charlie. "You're a friend whether you can swim or not."

Will came to Charlie's home for lunch, a real venture for him. The meal started with a large serving of papaya. Charlie's dad asked Will his opinion on current restrictions of foreign business. Will smiled. "Gee, no one's ever asked me about my views on anything." He sat up straighter. "I think the Philippine government is right to set restrictions." He raised his voice and gestured with his arms. "They're trying to rebuild their country!" This stance was, of course, in direct opposition to his father.

Will appeared to grow taller, bigger, his deformed chest filled out.

The family continued their discussion about rebuilding after the war. The maids cleared the fruit plates. They brought a large platter of fried fish to the table, followed by a beautiful wooden bowl with a cover. Charlie breathed deeply. The serving bowl was made of sandalwood, its warm perfume filled the room.

"Here," said Charlie's mother smiling as she passed Will the wooden bowl, "Help yourself."

He removed the lid, steam floated out. As the vapor cleared, Will looked in.

"Rice!" he screamed, dropping the container. Jumping up, Will ran across to the living room. He sat on the rattan couch, crying, his face buried in his hands. Great wrenching moans mixed with his sniffles.

Charlie's mother pushed her chair back, standing up, she struck the table gong once loudly, calling the kitchen staff. She moved to the couch and put her arm around Will. Charlie's father sat on the other side of Will, gently holding his hand.

"Let it out, it's okay," he said.

They sat in silence as Will cried. The sobs and moans slowed. Charlie brought him some tissues.

"My brother...he..." whispered Will. "The rice....."

"It's okay..." said Charlie's mother, giving Will a hug.

Will continued, saying words, sometimes sentences, woven between sobs, moans, and wiping his nose.

Everyone stood around, waiting for the rice to be ready. Rice for the whole concentration camp, their one meal for the day The pot, an old oil drum, much too heavy for the women to lift it off the fire. Two teenaged boys selected for the job. Placing a pole through the handles, lifting the pot and carrying it off the fire. One of the boys stumbled and fell. He was my older brother. The pot tipped over and the rice spilled on the ground.

Will stopped telling the story and threw himself off the couch onto the floor. He curled himself into a ball and cried even harder. Charlie's father knelt down, placed his hand lightly on Will's shoulder. That touch seemed to calm him. He continued.

Everyone was shouting. A prison guard rushed over, seeing what had happened, picked up a shovel, and hit my brother in the face. He tried to stand but fell back on his knees, his face covered with blood. The guard, shouting obscenities, hacked at him, blow after blow. No one dared to move. The guard killed him, threw down the bloody shovel, and stomped off. Everyone was hungry, actually starving. People rushed in, dropped to the ground, and ate the spilled rice...some was splattered with my brother's blood.

Will, suddenly quiet, sat up, climbed onto the couch, and said in a determined voice, "I've got to get outta here! I hate the Philippines. The damaged people, the ruined buildings, the constant reminders of the war."

"Is there any place, any family, you could go live with?" asked Charlie's father.

"No, I don't... " Will answered. "But I gotta get out. My parents hate me 'cause I remind them of the Camps. I'm the age now my brother was then." Turning to Charlie he said, "They hate you 'cause you look like my older brother. You're the age my brother was when… They said I couldn't see you anymore. You're my only friend."

Charlie's mother spoke. "I've heard some of the parents talking about sending their kids back to the States for high school. Has there been any talk of that for you? Maybe you could go sooner."

"I haven't heard anything," said Will. He shifted his feet. "But," he said in a determined voice, "I could tell them."

Will stood up, a smile crossed his face. Digging into a pocket, he pulled out a small wallet and retrieved a wrinkled photograph. Two adults looked out from the color print. Each had a warm smile and a sparkle in their eyes. A teenaged boy, between them, grinned mischievously.

"That's my father's sister. After the war, we went back to the States and stayed with them for a while. Their son is now in high school, about to go off to college. They gave me this photograph."

Will paused again, thinking.

"Maybe I could go live with them. I think they have room, if they wanted me." He turned the photo over, revealing an address written in faded pencil. "I wish…"

"Would you like me to write to them?" Charlie's father asked.

"Oh, yes! Please. I really want to go. You could ask them to write to my parents and invite me. That way it's their idea, not mine."

Everyone stood in silence for a moment. Will reached in his pocket.

"Almost forgot. Here, this is for you." He handed Charlie a .50 cal machine gun shell, a tracer, the most prized treasure. And best of all, an unburned tracer. Actually, a dud, because it didn't ignite to illuminate the line of fire, showing the way to the enemy.

"I don't want it anymore, even though it may be from the gun that helped liberate the Concentration Camp. I'm through with that time of grief and sadness. No more reminders. No more machine gun shells. I want to live where people don't eat rice every day."

A horn honked.

"That's my ride. I gotta go," said Will, walking with a light and determined step to the front door.

He stopped, turned, and with a smile, said, "I've been looking for a way of life, life away from killing, and hatred."

Will paused. "Thanks," he said. "I have found it."

SOMEONE IS COMING

"What?"

"CAN'T YOU HEAR?"

"No, what is it?"

"DON'T KNOW, IT'S—"

"Are you sure?"

"NO, BUT I CAN HEAR IT."

"Hummm."

"I'LL GO LOOK."

"No, you stay here."

"CAN'T SMELL...WIND..."

"I still can't hear anything."

"MAYBE SOMETHING TO EAT"

"Is that all you ever think of?"

"YEP"

"Is it getting closer?"

"I THINK SO."

"What are we going do?"

"IF THEY'RE FRIENDLY, I'LL WAG"

"I too will smile."

"I'LL SING THEM A SONG OF MY PEOPLE"

10TH MONTH

"Set'er up," said the contractor, "Another round for the new father-to-be."

"What's that silly grin on your face?" asked the foreman.

"I uh, I'm not used to drinking so…you know…so many beers." He sat down, or rather, collapsed on the bar chair, lay his head on the table, knocked over a couple of empty beer glasses, and passed out.

"Someone call his wife. He's in no condition to drive home, especially a bike."

"Hope she gets here quick," said the foreman, "before she pops the kid. Any day now."

So ended the New Year's Eve party, thrown by the contractor to celebrate the beginning of a week off from work. Also, the announcement of the impending birth of his son, due the first week of January.

But it didn't happen. Days, and then weeks passed.

It was okay with him, gave him more time to sculpt, humming *Here Comes The Sun* the new Beatles song to himself. He changed sun to "Son." This was his agreement with his wife. He would do construction work during the summer while she stayed home. In the winter, she would teach, and he would become the househusband taking care of their home and her two kids from a previous union. He had a few hours a day to sculpt while the three "girls" were off to school. But this winter she was pregnant.

They had both wanted a child, perhaps he more so. Conception had taken many more months than expected, raising questions. Was she no longer fertile? Was he infertile? They kept very accurate records of her monthly cycle. The first week in January was definitely the due date.

The first month of the new year unfolded slowly. Her doctor said everything was just fine. He questioned their record keeping.

She grew bigger, became more awkward, and slept during the day. Discussions about home birth disappeared. Winter rains set in. It was hard for her to exercise, even to go out. He watched as she tried to get up from the bed, her bulk pressing down into the mattress. She accepted his help standing up and walking to the bathroom. Back in bed, he rubbed her legs and back. The baby responded to his caresses with kicks. He was happy.

Here comes the son...It's alright...

Images of pregnancy filled his mind, wanting to be expressed in sculpture. Some were the smooth, beautiful curves of the female body. More and more often, with the continued struggles of the heavy pregnancy, other images crowded his consciousness. In everyday life, it seemed that things stopped working. The wax he was sculpting with was either too hot or too cold. His stepdaughters fought with each other. And the smooth curves of his sculptures took on a rough quality.

The motorcycle was not large, but it was fast. In the past, when he felt frustrated, he would go for a ride to clear his mind. The speedometer went to 120 mph, a challenge to make the needle hit the peg. The highway in the valley had a straight stretch over a mile long, easy to look out for traffic or the Highway Patrol.

He rolled the motorcycle out from under the deck. It would not start; the coil must have gotten wet. A simple solution: take the coil off and put it in a warm oven for an hour. But where could he find an hour? He put the bike away. Returning to the studio, his mind filled with the image of his wife's heavy tenth month. He did not return to his construction job.

One day, well into February, he helps her to the bathroom. When she emerges, she's very pale.

"Let's go," she says. "It's time."

The doctor instructs him to sit by the mother's head and wipe her face with a cool cloth. A mirror is set up so he can watch the birth, an innovation. He's only the second father to be allowed into the delivery room.

Here comes the son…it's alright…

They had talked over and over about the whole birth process, and along with his various reading, he felt prepared for the event.

"You must leave the room immediately, if and when I tell you to," says the doctor. "I don't want to deal with an upset father when he sees a little blood."

"Of course," the father says. "I know what to expect."

Minutes and hours take too long. Looking in the mirror he sees the baby's head crowning, he suddenly feels very cold, and lightheaded.

"I'm going to faint," he says.

Here comes the son …It's alright…

The young man crouches, places his face down on the cool tile floor, and passes out.

"Hey!" says the doctor. "Nurses get back here. I need you! He's alright, just let him come to."

"Congratulations," says the doctor as he enters the waiting room, "You have a healthy ten-pound baby, and the mother is doing fine. We had to do a little repair work down there, but she's okay. Go down to the viewing room and get a look at your daughter."

The new father slumps into a chair, his head buried in his hands. The doctor places his hand on the shoulder of the sobbing man.

"It's going to be alright," says the doctor, as he turns to leave. "She's going be just fine. Just a few stitches."

"Daughter?" asks the young man to the empty waiting room, "Where is my son? Damn it, damn. Damn. I'm surrounded by female energy; two stepdaughters, two female dogs, even the horse is a mare."

A feeling of despair overwhelms the young man, his hopes and dreams shattered. Images of doing "guy things" together, blown apart. Teaching his son how to use tools, and how to fly fish. Gone. Walking down the darkened hall, he stops at the viewing window. There are three or four small beds on the other side of the glass. Above each bundled baby is a sign. One reads:

sex: F
weight: 9 lb. 15 oz.
mother: his wife's name
father: his name

FATHER, that's me…

A soft blue light radiates from the tiny bundle. It grows in size and intensity The glow expands through the viewing glass until it surrounds and embraces the father.

A voice comes into his ears, "Am I to stay, or go back?" He feels it in his head.

"It is your choice. I am not completely in this world. You have a little time. Your decision."

He feels... no, he experiences with his whole being the murmuring energy within the light.

There is a tug in his heart.

Stay, it says.

He feels joy; he is wrapped in love; he is at peace.

For the next weeks, the father takes care of the infant. Rocking her back to sleep in the night, endless diaper changes, carrying her to the mother to be nursed, and then of course another diaper change. When the need arises, he carries the mother to the bathroom. It takes time for her to heal.

Once the thought of going for a motorcycle ride crowds into his mind.

"Nope," he says. "I'm a father now."

One morning, at first light, father carries baby out and sits on a porch bench. The sky is free of clouds, but the air is chilly. Father opens his down jacket and holds the baby next to his heart. The coat wraps around and covers them both.

"Maybe the winter rains are over," he says. "We'll be able to go on more walks. I'll take you to the beach and show you the Pacific Ocean."

He looks down at his daughter. Their eyes meet, she reaches up and grabs his beard, they both smile.

Rays of morning light peek over the trees and illuminate the yard, the house, and the porch. Its warmth surrounds the father holding his baby daughter.

Here comes the sun…It's alright

Tenth Month, 9.5" tall, bronze and granite

WEE SMALL VOICE

ME…me…me…*look at me!* The shouts reverberated inside my head. The stones, the blocks of marble, strewn about in the field were talking to…no, they were wailing to me. A few stayed quiet. Some whispered in a wee small voice. Others shone, catching my attention, with a white brilliance, brighter than the Italian sun above. Below me, the town of Pietrasanta defined by the Apuan mountains of solid marble.

I am selecting marble to fill my order of five tons, a container load, enough for my own use and some to sell from my studio in California.

The stone supplier informed me that I needed to select a few more blocks to fill my order. Everything was quiet in the field, no stones calling out. I walked past a pile of large blocks and crouched on one knee. The end of a very bright white stone enticed me. I reached in and touched it. The surface was both smooth and rough, both soft and hard, and felt both warm and cool. It was mine. The stone supplier informed me that it was his best block of Statuario sculpting marble. He was keeping it hidden under the pile, waiting for the right artist. Six-feet-tall, and weighing over one and a half tons, it cost as much as all the rest of my order, but I knew that I had to take it home.

"The stone talks to me," was my easy answer to a variety of questions about sculpting. There was more to it than that quick answer.

Stone did talk to me when I sculpted in marble and granite. There was a constant dialogue with the material being shaped. The communication was not easy to hear. The message might not come as sound in my ears, but in my heart or in my head, or maybe in my hands.

The creative process often started at the granite quarry. I would be looking for the size and shape of stone in which to render my idea. Sometimes, a nondescript boulder would shout at me from a pile of others, saying, "Look at me!" and I could see my finished sculpture within it. Other times, without an image in my head, a stone would whisper in a seductive tone, "See what I have." There, standing before me, was a beautiful, finished sculpture, a completely new idea. This new image excited me. Where did it come from? I knew that all I had to do was to do it. There was an urgency to take this block back to my studio and start work on this new sculpture, its image having come from somewhere.

Squaring off the bottom, standing up the future sculpture, I worked as quickly as I could. Always looking for ways to work faster, trying new tools and new techniques was also an important element in my creative process. I contracted with a company to fabricate diamond cutting and grinding tools to my specs. My secret was how fast I could create and render a sculpture in very hard granite.

Now that I'm writing, typing with a stick clutched between my bent fingers, it's time to explore more fully the loss of my connection with stone. A loss that brings tears to my eyes, and a tightness in my chest when I stand in the presence of my old sculptures. I remember and experience again the connection we had creating together.

In the past, I was often embarrassed by my uncontrollable up-welling of emotion, by the quivering in my voice, when interacting with a sculpture. This included talking about one, or standing and touching one, or even having a memory. Communicating with words became difficult. There was so much to express, but words were not my first language. The sculpture was my expression.

A 12th-century Japanese poet seemed to have shared this feeling.

> *I do not know what is here,*
> *but my tears flow in gratitude.*
> —*Saigyo*

I have spent a lifetime learning to *know,* to understand *what is here.* A lifetime of hearing the Wee Small Voice. A commitment to accepting and integrating the messages into my being. Marble and granite did talk to me, sometimes from the stone itself, and sometimes from the surrounding world.

It did not work for me to keep a log or diary of my interactions with the stone I was sculpting. It proved to be impossible to put the messages from the stones into words; they were too complex to describe. I did not even create a sketch to begin a sculpture. After all, a drawing is only two dimensions, but a stone is three.

Or does it have another dimension?

I was able to sense or see a view from all sides of the stone. What the other side looked like was clear to me. This included being inside the solid mass. From this vantage point, I could experience in my own body the emotion of the figure I was creating. It's hard to describe this ability, this way of seeing, this way of the stone talking to me.

I wanted to create a sculpture expressing the union of the Earth Mother and the Sky Father. Before I began "Primal" I had the image in my mind. In the sculpture, the female figure ascends from the sphere, being the Earth Mother. The Sky Father, male figure, descends. His right arm reaches high into the sky. Embracing the Mother, his face pressed into her left breast, she pulls him to her chest and heart with her left arm. He tries to continue and complete the embrace.

I had created the sphere of the earth and the strong right side connecting with the sky. Becoming the male figure myself, I buried my face into her left (feminine) side of breast and heart. It felt right. Moving my left arm around to complete the embrace, she grasped my elbow.

My whole sculpting body shifted and I became the Earth Mother. I felt the connection with the globe below me. The closeness of the male was good. But I did not want to be dominated. I held his arm with a strong gesture of both "come closer...stay away." The dialogue between the two figures, definitely male and female, was very loud and clear to me as I carved the marble. I had become each figure. The stone talked to me, not in words but in images with very powerful emotions.

Although the hard work of sculpting was enjoyable, I'm relieved that it's no longer a part of my life. My doctor questioned why the cartridge in my left knee was healthy but was completely gone in my painful right knee. I had been supporting a large machine, a saw with diamond teeth, on my right hip and knee, guiding and thrusting the cuts into the stone. It weighed thirty-five pounds but could cut very deep and very fast. However, it took its toll on my body.

Memories of the hard work do not bring tears to my eyes. Sometimes the images of developing a tool that made stone sculpting faster and easier do affect me. Where did these new ideas originate? Did the stones themselves tell me? What is it about the creative process that so deeply touches me and causes *"my tears to flow in gratitude."*

Behind my tears, there is a strong feeling of joy that can only be described as awe. Can all this: the stones talking, the creativity, the being at one with the whole process, and listening to the Wee Small Voice, actually be a glimpse of and a connection with the divine?

Primal Earth and Sky
female and male
45" tall. Statuario Marble

THE THREE GRACES

LOSS

The tree is almost down. Or as the arborist said, 'felled.'

It's almost noon, and off to one side is a huge pile of logs and branches, some as big around as a man's leg. The trunk, the central strength of the tree is still standing, defiant in its nakedness without its protective branches. Its weakness is also exposed. A long gash on the trunk from when a huge branch tore away and exposed its very heart. Disease took hold in the wound, slowly, methodically destroying the tree. The arborist had done what he could over time. It was not enough.

Caleb stands on the side porch watching, the sputtering roar of the chainsaws and their sickening sweet exhaust smell surrounds him. He wants to go inside, but feels he must stand witness to the final minutes of the tree's life.

The *Tree of Life,* a vital symbol in every major culture, East and West. He is witnessing the death of *Life.* The tree had been a part of life for Caleb's family, generation after generation. His grandmother, or was it his great grandmother brought the small seedling tree back from her travels in Asia or Southeast Asia before the war. Caleb couldn't remember which war. The grandmother built a house near the tree, protecting it from the cold north winds of winter. The south wall of the house was stone, which absorbed the day's sunlight, and radiated warmth to the tree through the night.

Over the generations, mothers would sit in the shade under the tree, nurse their babies, and play with their toddlers. Caleb's own son and daughter had been nurtured there, close to the tree.

That original grandmother had requested, upon her death, to be wrapped in a plain linen shroud and buried beneath "her" tree. The tree grew very well. Perhaps too well. Its roots grew under the foundation of the house, lifting and cracking the stone wall above.

Caleb wondered how many relatives had been laid to rest under the tree. No one in his generation, that he could remember, was actually buried there. Now, family members spread the ashes of their loved ones. Caleb's own wife, Grace, was there. He knew that she was not really there, just her ashes. She died young. Maybe the cancer had been triggered by the death of their son. He had joined a United Nations peacekeeping force and was deployed in Southeast Asia. The young man had hated war, the killing of people, the destruction of the world, and its ecosystems.

"Maybe," he had said, smiling, before he left, "I can save people, as well as the forests."

Caleb's wife Grace had been in Europe visiting their daughter and planned to stay to help with the first grandchild, when the news came that their son was missing in action. He and his platoon had gone into the deep jungle, and not returned. The body was never found. The night the news arrived, a tremendous storm hit the area. Downed power lines, uprooted trees, and flooding ravaged the area. Was this climate change? The next morning, checking for damage, Caleb saw the deep, devastating wound left in the tree when a large branch was ripped off. It lay on the ground. Its contorted shape, no longer a beautiful branch, lay very still in the mud. He imagined his son, laying very still in the mud of a far-off forest. Caleb felt the tree's oozing gash deep in his own heart.

His efforts to reach Grace failed, everything was down. He felt very alone. Using his chainsaw, he cleaned up the debris left by the storm. The branch no longer looked like his son. But staring at the open scar on the tree, which was dripping a blood red sap, Caleb could feel the damage painfully thrust into his whole being.

A few days later, his wife was able to reach him. She was very excited; they had a granddaughter! Everyone was doing fine. The news of the storm had not reached her, must have been a local anomaly. Caleb did not respond.

"Caleb," she said, "Are you still there? What's going on? Are you alright? Talk to me."

"Our son is missing, and presumed dead." He let out a deep groan. "It's not right. A child is not supposed to die before his parents."

His wife came home, and together they struggled to rebuild their lives. They were both hurting, each in their own way. Both did what could be done to help the other. But life was out of balance. A year later, they planned to go visit their daughter and her new family, hoping to ease their pain. Their doctor had found the cancer during routine physical exams. Caleb was thankful that they went ahead with their trip. It was the last time.

The months after their visit went by very fast or very slow, depending on their state of health. The arborists did what he could to save the tree. Each season there seemed to be less and less new growth. He tried to explain that trees, like us, have a life expectancy. And after all, this tree, growing in and adapting to a different environment had done exceptionally well.

Grace was not doing well. She died. He spread her ashes around the tree and in front of the deep scar where the branch had been torn out. That was a year ago. The tree had seemed to give up. Its time had come. Caleb wondered how soon his time would come.

The arborist came around to the side porch, interrupting Caleb's memories, and said, "I want to show you something. We've already cut across the scared, damaged part of the trunk. The wound was deeper than we thought." He looked back towards the tree. "We're ready to make the final cut. The stump will be just above the surface of the surrounding soil. I want you to see what I suspect."

The two men approached the tree, the chainsaw was just finishing the last cut. The remaining tree trunk toppled over, the squat stump lay bare. Caleb and the arborist stepped forward. The whole inside of the stump was punky, rotten to the core.

"Well," said the arborist, "That explains a lot. It's like the rot, the cancer, ate out the very heart of the tree."

"Thanks," said Caleb, turning away, hiding his face, going to the house, closing and locking the door behind him.

The next morning, a shaft of bright sun awakened Caleb, sleeping in his favorite recliner chair. The sunbeam flowed through a small window in the stone wall. Up to now the opening to the sun had been blocked by the branches and trunk of the tree.

Caleb struggled, trying to extract his body from the deep recesses of the chair. He fell back into the chair, taking his time to wake up. It had been an intense last two days. Yesterday, the felling of the tree. The day before, the family reunion. So many people had come, he was surprised. He wondered who had organized the gathering. He had just mentioned to someone that the tree was coming down, and if anyone wanted to say goodbye, now was the time.

A folding chair had been set up for him next to the tree. People came, said "hello" then touched the tree. Some laid a hand on the tree for a brief moment. Others, put their arms as far around the tree as they could. Some cried.

"Hi, Uncle Caleb," a teenager, a girl said, "I brought you a plate of food and a glass of iced tea."

He thanked her and smiled, wondering who she was. Was he really her uncle, or was that a polite way of addressing an older relative? It was awkward eating from a paper plate, but he managed. People had spread out blankets on the grass and were talking, laughing, and sharing food. So many people, he could recognize only a few.

Caleb slumped in his chair. All these people, but he was alone… and feeling loneliness. He felt like escaping, retreating into his house…a sanctuary, a place where he could look for balance.

A woman approached him, smiling. She was attractive, short auburn hair with some gray and cinnamon, and her smile made little wrinkles around her eyes.

"Hello Caleb," she said, extending her hand. "How are you doing? Lotta stuff here today. This spot reeks of memories. Oh, don't get up, I'll just sit on the grass. Do you want me to take your plate?"

They had chatted for a while. Caleb felt awkward. She looked familiar, but he couldn't remember her name or their relationship.

"I gotta go," she said standing up, "I'll see you again."

"I would like that," Caleb said, standing up and taking her hand. "Soon I hope."

Caleb continued struggling to get out of his recliner. It was comfortable but hard to get out of and stand up. Looking at the clock above the kitchen counter, it was much later than he thought. He started the coffee maker with four cups, that way he would have some for the afternoon. A quick shower woke him up. As he was drying himself he heard a knock on the door. Assuming it was the stump removal crew, he wrapped himself in a towel and opened the front door.

"Good morning, Caleb…Oh dear!" said a woman, the one from the party, "You said 'soon' but, I didn't know how soon. Sorry, I'll come back…"

"No, no. Please come in. I'll just finish dressing."

Caleb quickly returned, dressed in jeans, the shirt he had worn the day before, and slippers. Hair brushed. A smile on his face.

"Well," she said with a twinkle in her eyes, "Hello again. That coffee smells very good. Would you happen to have an extra cup?"

"Yes, in fact, I was just getting ready to take a cup myself, and go sit in the sun." He sat two mugs on the counter near the sugar bowl. "Will you bring the half 'n half from the fridge?"

"Of course," she said. "And I have fresh pastries to go with the coffee."

"Thanks, I was going to have granola for breakfast."

They sat on the covered porch, the morning sun warming them. Caleb broke the silence, explaining that he was embarrassed for not remembering her name and their relationship.

"Oh Caleb, that's okay," she said turning in her chair to face him. "I'm Isha."

She continued, explaining that she had been married to one of his cousins. Also, she and his wife Grace had babies at the same time.

"Yeah, now I remember," Caleb said, "I was so young, kids came so quickly, and I was away much of the time."

"Yes, that's true," said Isha. "But then I moved away, a messy divorce, and so on. The news of your son's death, the baby I helped raise, it was just too painful coming back."

"I'm very happy you came back."

"There's more," Isha said. "Grace and I kept in touch. I wanted to come but got involved in legal stuff. My daughter's grandparents gave her a house, after their son, her father, died of an overdose. We just moved here only a few weeks ago."

"That's quite a story," said Caleb

"Yeah," said Isha. "But I have to…you know." She stood up and went inside.

Caleb took her absence to do a quick search on the name "Isha"

He greeted her return with, "AH, Isha, the one who protects and gets the job done!"

She stopped, staring at him. "How did you know, and what else do you know?"

"I just looked it up on my phone. Why, what more—?"

"I promised not to tell, but now…" Tears pooled in her eyes.

She explained that she had contacted Grace, and over the years they had tried to work out a visit.

"As the end drew closer," Isha said. "Grace had asked me to "protect" you, Caleb, when she…"

Isha was trying to hold back tears. Caleb reached over and held her hand. A moment later he withdrew his hand. There was a spot on his back that was so irritating. He had to scratch it.

"Thanks," he said. "Might be nice…protect. But how?"

"But what can I do?" asked Isha. "Do you really need protection, you seem so competent."

Caleb reached out to take her hand again but stood up, and started to shuffle around the porch. "Well…" He stopped his pacing, backed up to a corner post, and began to scratch his back. "Sorry, I was just trying to answer your question. All of a sudden, I got this itch…Can't quite reach it." Caleb laughed, "What I really need is 'protection' from whatever is chewing on me."

"Whew," Isha said. "That's easy. I was afraid you might want me to…Here, turn around. You looked like a big bear scratching on a tree."

She reached up under his shirt and stopped. "Is this the spot?" Pulling out her hand, she held a small chip of wood.

'Look," Caleb said. "It's a piece of green wood. Must'a come from the last chainsaw cuts, yesterday. You know, the little part of the stump still trying to live."

Isha reached up and placed her hand on his back.

"There, up a little, right there," said Caleb, removing his shirt. "It still itches. Please scratch it, just between the shoulder blades.

"Is that it?" she asks.

"Oh, thanks. That feels so good."

"Caleb," asked Isha. "Do you know what a chakra is?"

She moved around to be in front of him. The sun behind her shone through her hair. The red cinnamon color had an intensity of its own.

"Well…Ummmmm"

"The body has seven energy points, from the base of the spine to the top of the head." Isha paused, stepping closer to him. "This green chip, this annoying itch, was pinpointed on the central chakra, the heart. Its accompanying color is green."

"Oh!" Caleb said, "Why? What is it trying to say?"

"And you know what?" Isha said. "It will keep itching until you listen to what it has to say." She was smiling.

"How should I do that? I'll go online, and…"

"No, don't do that. Just get a general idea of chakras. You could study for a lifetime and still not know everything. Wait until one 'bites' you. Then study that specific one. Listen to the wee, small voice. You will understand."

"Excuse me," came the voice of the arborists as he came round the corner of the house, "There's a car parked in the driveway. I need to bring up the stump grinder."

Caleb was embarrassed, standing there with his shirt off and a woman so close.

Isha didn't miss a beat.

"Go get a clean shirt," she said, "This one's filled with sawdust. No wonder you were itching. I'll move my car."

He made a hasty retreat into the house.

When Caleb returned, Isha announced she was taking him away from the noise and pain of his tree's death. She drove. "We need to be near water…It helps with the emotions. You know, helps to quiet their raging."

"There's a lake near here," Caleb said. "We could—"

"I know, that's where we're going."

"Let's stop for a late breakfast, or early —"

Reaching over to pat Caleb's leg, Isha said, "It's taken care of. Remember, my job is to take care of you."

"Oh, I thought you were supposed to protect me."

"I am."

They drove along in silence. Caleb noticed a number of signs marking, 'Beach Access' which Isha passed by. He decided to relax and enjoy being 'protected' for the day. She turned off the highway and down a dirt lane, stopping at a rustic log cabin on the lakeshore.

Caleb lowered his window and breathed in the earthy scent of forest pine-pitch, carried on a gentle breeze. The heaviness of the last few days was trying to worm its way through the pleasure of the moment. Isha reached over and held his arm. With that, she broke the film of darkness which was creeping over him.

"Listen to me," she said, taking his hand in both of hers. "I don't want to come across as being bossy or pushy, but it's my nature to get things done, to take charge. So here we are."

The cabin door opened, and the girl who had brought him a lunch plate came out to the car. "Hi, Uncle Caleb. Welcome to my home."

As she stepped into the sunlight, Caleb noticed that she had red-gold hair pulled back in a ponytail. Her mother's hair was more reddish brown, or auburn.

"Let me introduce my daughter, Grace," said Isha. "Yes, I named her after my best friend, your wife."

"Very happy to meet you," said Caleb, getting out of the car. "And thanks again for the plate of food. Saved the day."

"You're welcome. It was Mom's idea. She sent me ahead to see if you were approachable. You seemed to be so wrapped up with the death of your tree, and everything…"

"I am so thankful you judged me—"

Grace shook her head. "No, not judged, just checking you out."

Isha took Caleb's hand. He felt a flutter in his heart. She said, "Let's all go in. We have a lot to talk about."

"Bye Mom," said Grace stepping onto her moped. "I'm going for my sailing lesson. Be back for dinner."

"Have a great time," said Isha. "Oh, will you pick up a small container of half 'n half? We may have company for dinner."

"Do you sail?" asked Caleb. "So do I. My boat is—"

"That's great. Gotta go, talk later. Bye."

Still holding his hand, Isha led the way into the house. "This really is Grace's house, but it's complicated. Her father's parents gave it to her when…" her voice trailed off. "Anyway, we're living here now. It would be great if you could meet her where she's at. And at this moment, at age thirteen, that's sailing."

Still hand in hand, they walked down to the lake and out on the pier to a bench at the end. Caleb was surprised and pleased to see a floating dock tied below.

"You know," said Caleb. "I could bring my boat over and tie to the dock. That way Grace, the boat, and the lake are in the same place. After a few times sailing, she could take the boat out by herself. It's good for a kid to experience, to have that gut feeling of being the captain of one's ship."

"That would be so great!" Isha said.

"For me too. I haven't been sailing for a long time. The boat is put away in my garage, needs some TLC."

"Don't we all," Isha added, nodding her head.

They sat on the bench not talking. Caleb relaxed, the warm sun melted his tension. He looked out over the lake and thought about sailing with Isha, a smile lit up his face. More images of being with her continued. Caleb hoped his fantasies were not being shouted out by his body language or by the way he looked at her.

Caleb stayed for dinner. It was delicious. He realized he had missed home cooked meals. This only added to the details of his very active thoughts. After supper, Caleb wondered if Isha was going to invite him stay the night. She didn't. She just drove him home.

In the night, after his usual 3:00 am trip to the bathroom, Caleb returned to thinking about Isha. He was surprised at how vivid his fantasies were. She was beautiful, had a nice smile, a twinkle in her eyes. And…after all, it had been a long time since he had been intimate with a woman. Caleb also realized he liked being taken care of. Suddenly, he sat up straight. *What would it be like to live with a teenager?* He had already been there, done that. He loved his daughter, but raising a teenager had been difficult for both he and his wife. *Do I really want to do that again?*

For two weeks, Caleb helped Isha finish moving in. He hung pictures, unstuck cabinet drawers, and made himself useful. They had time to talk. Sometimes walking on paths around the lake. Often taking a sandwich lunch out to sit on the pier. They grew comfortable with each other.

Suddenly, after one such lunch, Isha jumped up and said, "I'm hot, I'm going for a swim. You too."

"I don't have a swimming suit," said Caleb.

Isha started taking off her clothes. "Ever hear of skinny dipping?" she said through the Tee shirt slipping over her head. Caleb couldn't move, he just sat and watched. She ran down the ramp leading to the dock below. Caleb looked, or more precisely, stared at the many beautiful female curves bouncing and shimmering until they disappeared in a splash of water.

Caleb quickly stripped, using the moment of privacy while she was underwater to free himself from the entanglement in his boxer shorts. Running down the ramp, he tried to cover himself with one hand. Jumping in, he found he could just barely stand on the sandy bottom, his head out of water.

Isha swam over to him and reached out to hold his shoulder. She was too short to stand on the sandy bottom.

"It's deeper on the other side of the dock."

"You must have been reading my mind," said Caleb, "I was just thinking about bring my boat into the dock."

Isha slipped both arms around his neck.

"I love reading your mind, and I know what else you're thinking." Her long legs wrapped around his waist. He reached down to hold her hips.

"It's time," she said, her lips near his ear, "to start a new chapter."

The cold water's effect on his body changed the scenario he was progressing into. They both laughed.

"My bed is much warmer and more comfortable," Isha said, "And we have the whole night."

"I'm hungry," Isha said. "Let's make dinner."

The phone rang while they were chopping veggies.

"It's Grace," Isha said to Caleb. "She wants to stay over at a friend's." She turned back to the phone. "Of course you can. Thanks for calling. Why are you so late?…Oh." Isha turned to Caleb. "The race went long because the wind died. She wants to talk to you."

"Hi," said Caleb, taking the phone. "How was it? What boats do you race in?"

"Little El Toros. Uncle Caleb, when can you take me for a sail in your boat?"

"Soon, very soon," he replied. "We just need to pull it out of my garage, clean it up, and away we go."

"Oh boy!" she shouted. "How about tomorrow?"

Isha took back the phone. "We're just making dinner. Let's talk when you get home. Have a great time. 'Bye."

"Were you worried?" Caleb asked. "It was getting dark and—"

"No," replied Isha. "I don't worry. Worrying is like saying a prayer for what you don't want."

"Okay," he said. "But what do you do when, you know, when something comes along?"

"I visualize what I do want. I was aware it was getting late. I just pictured in my mind Grace calling, and she did."

"Sounds great," said Caleb, "if it works."

"It does, most of the time. It just takes practice. It's creating an image of what you want."

"I'm visualizing what I want," Caleb said, putting his arms around Isha and nuzzling her neck.

"Hummm," she said. "I think dinner can wait."

JOY

Caleb woke at first light. This was not his bedroom. It only took a moment to remember where he was. He smiled. Beside him was a sensuous, breathing (well, maybe quietly snoring) shape, covered with an early American quit. He slipped out of bed. After a shower, he intended to make his way back under the quilt, but the bed was empty. The smells of coffee and sausage filled the room. Another delicious scent teased Caleb. It was the sweet fragrance of hot fruit.

"Help yourself to coffee," Isha said. "One more batch of blueberry pancakes. Hope you slept well." Still holding the spatula, she gave him a quick kiss. "I certainly did."

The food was superb! Caleb could not remember the last time he had had blueberry pancakes, and sausage too. But he felt so tense, the butterflies in his stomach, the slight nausea …

Reaching over, and taking his hand in hers, Isha said. "It was wonderful last night. But I'm feeling a little awkward this morning."

"Me too"

"I know I promised to protect you, but from what? Sex-starved single moms?"

"We…I…"

"It's all happening so fast. We don't, we hardly know…"

"I know enough," said Caleb, "to keep exploring and learning, and…"

"You're sweet," Isha said. "But I've got to say something, to tell you…But I don't want to scare you away."

"You will not."

"Okay, well—"

The kitchen door flew open, Grace burst into the room. "Oh great!" she exclaimed with pleasure. "I'm glad you're still here. Can we get your boat now, please, please? We could tie it to the dock, and—"

"Grace," said Isha. "Don't be so pushy."

"Good idea," Caleb said. "I mean the part about tying to your dock, not about being pushy. Let's go back to my place and see about setting up my old boat. If all goes well, maybe a sail on the lake."

"Oh yeah! Let's go, let's go!"

"Okay," Caleb said. "Let's go and see what she needs, Haven't used it for a long time."

"Why?"

"My wife and I loved to sail together," said Caleb. "When she got sick, she could no longer…"

"Well," Grace said, "I can. Let's do it."

Inside the garage, broken furniture, ancient boxes, and other junk blocked the boat's exit.

"Let's clear this crap out of the way," Grace said. "Move the boat out, then put it all back where the boat was."

"But—"

"You don't need to put your boat back in here. You can keep it moored at my dock."

Well, okay, thought Caleb. *She seems to know what she wants and is making it happen. A lot like her mother.*

Caleb started the air compressor and brought the trailer tires up to pressure. Together, the two rolled the boat and trailer out into the warm sun. Using the air hose with a nozzle, Caleb started to blow the accumulated dust off the boat. After a few moments, he passed the blower to Grace. She was smiling, inspecting every surface and design.

"Next," Caleb said, "we need to wipe down the varnished bright work with a damp cloth."

They removed the canvas snapped over the cockpit, revealing the uncluttered, shipshape interior. Everything was carefully stowed. He noticed the "his and hers" pair of lifejackets, tucked under the port side seats. On the other side, his wife Grace's colorful windbreaker and her sailing hat sat waiting for her. Pressure built behind his eyes and his throat tightened. A sob wanted out. He left the cleaning to his teenage helper and retreated indoors to the bathroom. The tears came. Memories of sailing together flooded his mind, setting their course along a moonbeam at night. Trailering the boat to the coast and sailing in a tidal river, tasting the salt in the flung spray. And making love anchored in a secluded cove, laughing as they figured out what to do with their legs and the ever-present centerboard case.

No wonder he hadn't taken the boat out all these years.

Returning to the driveway, his helper was just finishing wiping down the beautiful, wine-glass-shaped transom. The varnished mahogany shined very bright in the sun.

"That looks great!" Caleb said. "All we have to do is shake out the sails to make sure no mice have nested in the folds. And, of course, check out the running rigging, you know, the halyards and the sheet lines."

"Yeah, I know." She paused for a moment, "The name on the transom, "Grace" is the same as your wife and also my name."

"I named the boat after my wife, and your mother said she named you after her best friend, also my wife."

"Awesome!" said Grace. "Then somehow this boat and I are related."

They stopped at the town's deli for a couple of sandwiches and bottles of water. Caleb drove onto the launching ramp. Together, they raised the mast and fastened the stainless-steel standing rigging. Grace, on one side of the boat, followed the lead of Caleb working on the other side.

"I've been thinking," Caleb said, "about changing this rig to a single-lug sail."

"Why?"

"Easier to set up, not all these steel cables."

"Yeah," said Grace, "But will it go to windward, you know, point up as well?"

"We'll see," Caleb said. "Racing is only one way of enjoying sailing."

The boat slipped into the water. Caleb went to park the trailer while Grace secured the mooring lines. Returning to the boat, he checked how Grace had cleated the mooring lines to the dock. "That's a good job of tying the boat. I'll show you another way, a way for a quick getaway. Not now, let's go sailing, next time."

Grace was grinning. "Next time, yeah."

Caleb raised the sails, letting them flap freely in the wind. Moving aft to take the tiller, he called out, "Stand by to cast off, stern line first."

"Aye, aye, sir!" Came a happy and excited response.

"Cast off. Give me a little push ahead for some steerage way. Remember to come aboard."

They both laughed as the boat came alive.

"Pull in the jib sheet… no, the other side. I know El Toros don't have jibs. You'll learn. That's too tight, let the sheet out a little. See the nice curve of the sail?"

"Oh God," thought Caleb. *"It feels so wonderful sailing again. It's been too long."*

Sailing away from the dock and out into the lake, Caleb made a variety of maneuvers, showing and explaining to Grace each move. She was totally focused.

"You ready to take the helm?" he asked.

"Who, me?"

"Yep"

The wind was fresh, just enough that both sailors sat on the high side to trim the boat.

"I'll tend to the jib, you just tell me what you want."

They changed places. Grace grasped the tiller so firmly that her knuckles showed white.

"Relax," Caleb said, "The tiller not going to get away. It works the same way as the tiller on an El Toro."

"Okay, okay," Grace said, taking a deep breath. "Where are we going?"

"You're the captain, you have the helm, you set the course. Eventually, we should make it home."

"Home?" asked Grace.

"Uh…I mean, your home." Caleb looked away.

Grace smiled. "Sounds good to me."

Grace made a number of maneuvers, trying different tacks and learning the boat.

"Uncle Caleb?" asked Grace. "Will you sit farther forward?"

"Sure, am I crowding you?"

"No, not really. It's just, well, there's too much weight in the back. We're dragging our tail. The Center of Resistance is too far aft. It may not make so much difference in your boat, but in an El Toro the placement of the weight is very important. The boat must be in balance to sail right."

"You really have a feeling for the boat, that's wonderful," Caleb said. "Let's see if you can handle the jib by yourself. You'll need to if you're going to sail alone."

Grace was making a number of practice tacks, when Caleb spotted a brightly colored beach ball bobbing in the water ahead.

"Let's make a 'man overboard' maneuver on that ball."

They "saved" the ball on their third attempt.

"I love sailing," Grace said. "It's like I can feel it in my bones. It's…it's, I just can't put it into words. Thanks so much for taking me out."

"Well, you're welcome. I wonder how much longer this boat would have sat in the garage if you hadn't pushed me to go out. There's another item that I would like to share with you. It was written by a fellow sailor I know."

Caleb rummaged through a watertight locker and found a printed card. He handed it to Grace.

YOUR POWER

Keep one hand on the tiller, the other grasps the sheet.

Through the tiller and the rudder,
You have touched all the waters of the world.

Holding the sheet, and adjusting the sail
You have made contact with the winds of the world's air.

You are in control of these two great fluids of the earth.

You are the captain of your ship.

You are co-creating with the earth.

Feel the power between
your hands, between your arms, across your chest.

Let this power flow through your heart
Claim it as your own.

—Welton Rotz

Caleb looked at Grace, her cheeks were wet. "That's it, that's it!" she said, "Oh God, Caleb you understand."

They grinned at one another.

"Let's see," she said, "how this boat sails off the wind." She steered the boat until the wind was over their backs.

"Be careful," said Caleb. "Don't let the wind get behind the sail, or it'll jibe and—"

"I know, I know. We do it all the time in the El Toros. Will you sit on the other side and lift the centerboard?"

"Okay," said Caleb, "but this boat has a much larger main sail. And remember you have a head sail."

Grace looked away from the sail and the wind to watch Caleb. Without warning, the wind caught the back side of the sail. It was thrown violently to the other side in an uncontrolled jibe.

Caleb, suspecting what might happen, ducked just in time to avoid being hit by the boom as it swung over. It just missed Grace.

The rigging whipped; the boat shuttered. Then it regained its course.

"The wind just came so suddenly," she said. "So much power!"

"Next time we sail," said Caleb, "I'll show you how to do a controlled jibe."

Grace continued sailing the boat to its new moorage on the floating dock with only a few suggestions from Caleb.

"I can tell by the grins on your faces that it was a good sail," Isha said, as the two sailors walked into the kitchen. "Hope you're hungry. I'm roasting a small turkey for dinner."

"Smells wonderful," Caleb said. "Just what a pair of sailors home from the sea need to complete a perfect day."

"It was awesome," Grace said. "I'll tell you all about it over dinner. But now, Uncle Caleb needs a ride into town to get his car and trailer."

During the drive, Caleb asked Isha what she meant to tell him the day before.

"Oh, that." She sighed. "This is such a great day. I'll tell you another time."

Over dinner, Caleb told Isha, "Grace is a natural sailor. A quick learner, in tune with the wind and the boat. I—"

"Caleb is the best teacher ever!" Grace interrupted with great enthusiasm. She added, "He even let me sail all the way home. And when we got close, he said I should bring the boat up to the dock. And I did!"

Isha flashed a proud smile at Caleb. Reaching out to lay her hand on Caleb's arm she said, "Thanks."

He pushed back his chair, put both hands on the table, and said, "I have decided to rename my boat."

"What?"

"Why?"

"Since my wife's name was Grace, and I named my boat GRACE after her, and *you*," he pointed at the teenager, "were also named after my wife, there seems to be a real connection. I have decided to rename my boat THE THREE GRACES."

"Oh!" the two women exclaimed in chorus. "Why?" they both asked.

"There are many definitions of The Three Graces. It's a favorite theme for paintings and sculpture. They all share the common elements of Beauty, Light, and Love. There's a balance, there's stability."

He paused, then added, "All the definitions, both religious and secular, agree that Grace cannot be earned. It is something that is freely given. You both, each in your own way, have given me so much. It's a rebirth after the death of my tree."

He rubbed his eyes. "This death took with it a lifetime of joys and sorrows. I'm grieving, grieving for the loss of my wife, the loss of my son, and the loss of my tree." Caleb wiped away a tear creeping down his cheek.

Isha dapped at her eyes, while Grace sniffled. They reached across the table to touch Caleb's arms.

BALANCE

Caleb pulled the collar of his coat tighter. This rain was cold, much more than the first rains of winter had been. He wondered if there would be snow. Not likely at this elevation, but still... Caleb finished checking the tie-downs on the tarp over the open cockpit of his boat, he knew there would be wind in this storm. The boat had not left the dock for over a month, even in good weather. Was it time to haul it out and return it to his garage?

Halfway back to the cabin, Caleb stopped. The wind had come up and was blowing him in the face, pushing him back, attempting to blow away his hat. He turned and looked back at the boat. With the wind, came the rain, and with the rain, sleet. It was painful making his way back to Grace's home. Again, he turned and saw the boat tugging and jerking against the mooring lines. Was the boat trying to leave? To get away? A thought, more like a visual image, crowded into his mind. He tried to push it away, but it stayed and became stronger. Returning to the cabin, Caleb built up the fire in the wood stove to push back the chill in the air.

With a mug of hot coffee, he pulled the chair close to the fire. His visual scenario superimposed itself onto the room, it would not go away. It was like watching a speeded-up movie in slow motion. It was all there, Grace's house was cold and crowded. Winter had brought a chill; all three of them suffered colds, one after another. There was bickering, usually over small things. Mother and teenage daughter fought. Caleb knew this was normal, having lived through it with his own daughter. But it still left tension in the home.

"You're not my father!" Grace had screamed, jumping up, running to her room, and slamming the door.

Caleb tried to remember what he had said to trigger this response. He thought he had been careful not to imply he was Grace's father. It was not easy living with a teenager.

Caleb admitted to himself that he was questioning his role in this house. There was a feeling of unbalance. The bedroom passion was diminishing. When one or the other had a bad cold, they did not sleep together. He missed the physical and emotional warmth they had shared. It seemed to him that Isha had shut down, had left the home. He also admitted that he had a great desire, maybe more like a deep need to have a home. Where was she? Where was home? What could he do? Returning the boat to his garage and workshop was one thing that he could do. Caleb had stopped by his house a few times, but it had been weeks since his last visit.

Resolving the logistics of the car, boat trailer, and the boat all arriving at the boat ramp, two miles away was a challenge. Grace did not want to sail the boat there, even though it would have made it much easier. Maybe she was afraid she was losing her connection with sailing. For a brief moment, Caleb thought that that "connection" was with him. Was she still mad at him?

He had, after all, given her a "father" she didn't have. Maybe she didn't want it. As soon as the storm passed, he would ask her again to go with him to return the boat.

The storm was over in a week, none too soon for Caleb. The weather made an abrupt change. It felt like spring. The sun was shining, and the breezes were warm. A week or so later, Grace was helpful but withdrawn during the whole process of relocating the boat. When he dropped her off at home he noticed tears on her face. He called out to her, but she didn't stop, just ran into her house, and slammed the door.

It was dark when he made it into his house. It had taken longer to move the boat into the garage than he had expected. The boat seemed to have grown larger and the garage grown smaller, and the piles of junk grown taller. The house was cold, damp cold.

Dinner was a can of chili, heated in the microwave and a beer he found in the back of the fridge. Caleb remembered that he had been vague in communicating with Isha his plans to stay at his house after moving the boat. The chili did not set well on his stomach, or maybe it was the old beer. He wondered what dinner she had prepared, and he was missing.

Caleb headed to bed early. The TV service had expired. The bed sheets were cold. He stumbled around looking for a blanket. Even after all those years in this house, this was not home. He felt adrift, tossing about in a storm. The image of his boat thrashing against its mooring lines continued to play and replay across the screen of his mind. What was it trying to tell him?

Caleb believed in that kind of stuff; that messages could be received, or heard if one would just pay attention. These were non-physical whispers coming from the physical world out there. All he had to do was to listen and to interpret. But what if he had made a mistake, had gotten it wrong? What if it was all a bunch of phony spiritual Woo Woo? Maybe the restless boat struggling against its restrictive mooring lines had not meant it was time to leave.

But then what did it mean?

The digital clock beside the bed advanced slowly. Caleb slipped into sleep only to awaken, check the time on the clock, and watch the boat struggling against its mooring lines in his mind's eye again. The storm in his image intensified. He could feel the wind and the sting of the sleet in his face. The pain which had caused him to look back at the boat. What was the meaning?

Caleb sank into sleep, only to be awakened again. The clock face was dark, the house was still, the furnace was quiet. He was cold, the power must be off. Pulling up the extra blanket, he tried without success to find a comfortable position. Throwing the blanket over his shoulders, he shuffled to the kitchen to check the time on the clock above the sink. The second hand was not moving, the battery was dead.

A fire started in the stone fireplace helped subdue the chill. Caleb pulled a chair close and sat, staring into the embers.

The nonphysical world was no longer whispering, it was shouting. He had to decipher the message. Closing his eyes, he asked for help. The disturbing image; still there.

The boat was wildly thrashing against the mooring lines, just like Caleb had seen when the wind and rain in his face caused him to turn and look back at the boat.

He made a conscious effort to change the troubling picture. In his imagination, Caleb created a new image. He added spring lines to the existing mooring lines on the boat, a new line from the bow all the way back attached to the dock near the end of the boat. Another line from the stern running forward to be cleated to the dock close to the bow. The boat settled down and quietly rode out the storm. It no longer surged forward and back, jerked by the shorter mooring lines. A balance was established between the turbulence of the storm and THE THREE GRACES.

Caleb sat and continued to enjoy the fire's warmth. He knew he had made the correct interpretation, to add more mooring lines. Not to cast off the ties, and sail away, but to add more connections. Connections that were flexible and had spring in them to help during rough times. The additional bonds gave balance within the relationship, within the home.

A loud knock came from the front door. Before he could stand, the door was thrown open and Grace rushed in. "I want you to bring the boat back!" she shouted. "You can't just cast off the moorage lines and sail away."

"I—" Caleb started to say.

Grace strode over and stood above Caleb, still sitting in his chair. She clenched her fists and continued shouting. "That boat belongs at my dock. It's got *my* name on it."

Caleb pushed his chair back and started to stand, only to fall back into the chair as Grace leaned closer. The sun had reached the small window high in the stone wall. The bright light shone on her hair which had escaped from its ponytail. The red-gold hair flew about her face, the fiery colors screaming.

She announced, her voice quivering, "I'll get a job and buy the boat if that's what it takes."

"You're right," he said, taking her hand. "That's where the boat belongs."

Grace slumped into a chair and buried her face in her hands. "Mom wants you to come back too." Her voice, a squeak.

Caleb responded softly, "Let's put your moped in my truck and go home."

Grace and Caleb walked side by side through the side yard on the way to his truck. He wondered if he should reach out and hold her hand.

"Stop," said Grace, grabbing his arm. "Look!"

There, shooting up from where the old tree's stump had been removed, was a miniature tree. It was only a few inches tall, but the leaves looked very much like the old one before. The warm morning sun made the little tree shine bright green. Caleb felt a tug, a jolt in his heart. He smiled.

"I thought I saw it on my way in," Grace said. "I was going to tell you. What are you going to do with it now?"

"I think Isha would like to hear the good news," Caleb said. "About the little tree and the boat." He felt the hold on his arm tighten.

"I'm going to ask her if the three of us could build a new family," he said.

Grace laid her head on his shoulder.

RED AND GREEN

I love to be on the water at night, sailing or powering. When the wind is down and the moon is up, it shines a shimmering path that begs to be followed. It's easy to set one's course, maybe even to the moon itself. On a dark night with no moon's path to follow, the restaurants in Jack London Square along the Alameda Ship Channel are enjoyable destinations. The Channel also houses international container shipping facilities, their monstrous cranes towering over the water. San Francisco Bay's heavy industry blazes with lights along the shoreline, multiplied by their reflections on the dark water.

With so many lights and the profusion of piers built out into the waterway, it's a challenge to determine one's route along this dog-legged waterway. The edges are not perceivable, too many bright lights on the shore, above it, and on the buildings behind. Only the pairs of red/green markers stand out proud from the multitude of glaring white lights.

Sailing from one pair of channel markers to the next is the only way to set your course past the looming cranes off-loading container ships. It's comforting to pass between the familiar pair of red/green marker lights, ("red right returning") and sail on to the next pair of markers.

But wait a minute! The next pair of red/green lights are higher above the water, way higher!

THERE ARE NO SHORELIGHTS SHINING BETWEEN!

The space between the lights is black, very scary black. There are no reflected shore lights on the water in front of me.

The lights are approaching closer, dead ahead.

Those are port and starboard running lights.

IT'S A SHIP!

I can hardly make my hands work. Everything slows down, except the looming hulk of the black ship. The water in the Channel turns to thick muck, sticking and holding back my little boat. My legs tighten, ready to run…but where? I feel cold, except for the warm wetness in my jeans. My hand grabs the throttle, my knuckles shine white even in the darkness.

Will the inboard diesel engine, which has been loafing along up to now, respond to the pressure on the lever in my hand? Just last week, or was it a month ago, the speed control jammed. I was gonna fix it, but the next time I went out, it was working okay.

The old marine engine, the one which is too big, too heavy, and has too many hours, roars to meet the challenge. My boat shutters, the prop kicks out a sizable wash. We move.

The ship passes behind me, so close I could have reached back and touched it.

ADAM'S FIRST WIFE

Three couples, six people, have just finished two large pizzas and several bottles of wine. The conversation has run the course of climate change, troubles in the Middle East, and national politics.

The host, Morey, stands and clears the table. The conversation shifts to the role of the "man" in a domestic relationship. A few jokes are cracked. The host laughs and continues clearing.

"We're too old for this," Morey says. "Everyone here has been divorced."

All eyes turn to Mary and Ed. Everyone knows that their marriage is under stress, with divorce an obvious cloud on the horizon. They aren't even sitting next to each other. That will be a second divorce for Ed and a third for Mary.

"Why," she asks, her face tight with unshed tears. "Is it so hard to make a relationship work? Both want it, but..."

"I don't know," Susan says. "But my parents lived in a time and place where divorce was a sin. I grew up in that marriage hell and escaped into a marriage as soon as I could. That, of course, ended." Turning to her husband and taking his hand, she said, "We're making 'us' work."

"Of course," Morey says, "divorce is difficult, but so is life."

"Even Adam," Bill says, "had a first wife."

"What?" the group exclaims. "I've never heard of that!"

"You mean," Bill says, "they didn't tell you in Sunday School?"

"I'm Jewish," Morey says. "I never heard it either."

Bill unfolds the ancient story. Adam, created by God, was unhappy. He wanted a mate like all the other animals. When a woman appeared, Adam tried to mount her from the back as he had observed in nature.

"The woman turned," Bill says, "and slapped Adam. She said that they were in a relationship and would meet face-to-face. Adam couldn't understand and tried to force her."

The group around the table nods with understanding.

"What happened then?" asks Jane, remembering an experience she had.

Bill pauses as if to build tension around his story. He chooses his words carefully. "She turned her head, and with a toss of her hair, walked away."

"Then what?" asks someone.

"Well," Bill says, "According to the Gilgamesh Epic, Adam sulked over his beer, or whatever he was drinking, and begged God to give him another, more submissive, woman. And Eve appeared."

One of the men smacks his hand down on the table. "Yep, I can understand that."

He immediately receives a jab in his ribs from his wife, who asks what happened to Lilith.

"She shows up in the fertile crescent, becoming the Great Mother of all the pre-Biblical people," Bill answers.

"Wasn't she depicted as a she-devil in some early Jewish writings?" someone asks.

"Yes," Bill responds. "She was depicted along with all the, quote 'evil deities' of the foreign people. She received a great deal of bad press."

"Isn't she called 'The Night Witch' in some modern Jewish writing? Why?" a woman asks.

"I know," Ed says, "She visits me at night when I'm on a business trip. It's very disturbing. When I wake up my sheets are wet." He looks across the table. "I wish my wife were with me those nights."

"Me too," Mary says, her voice just above a whisper. "I suspected you were with another woman. I didn't know it was Lilith."

"I'm going to Chicago next. Would you like to come along?" Ed asks. "There's a lot for you to do while I'm in my meetings. And at night—"

"Oh, wow!" Morey interrupts. "A threesome."

His wife kicks him in the shins under the table.

"Ow!"

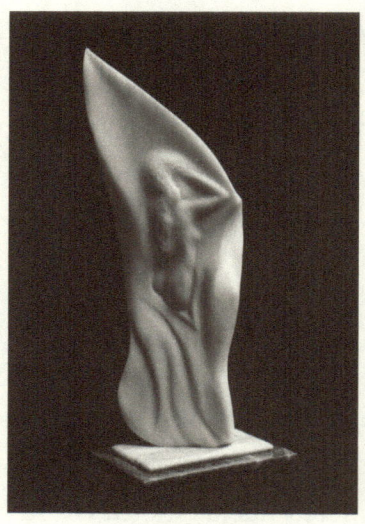

Lilith
10" tall. Portugues Pink Marble

ERASER

"Excuse me, what is that thing?" An attractive twenty-something woman at the next table asks. My wife and I have ordered coffee in a street-level atrium in NYC, where we're surrounded by Claes Oldenburg's sculptures. The show includes the recognizable huge paper clip, the very tall clothespin, and a few more. "That thing" stands about seven feet tall. It is a reproduction of a ten-foot-tall original Oldenburg artwork. Three elements make up the sculpture. A large, reddish-pink disk stands on its edge, about three-feet tall and 3 ½ inches thick. A bright metal clasp straddles the disc, attached through the center axle. Sprouting out of the top of the metal saddle is a four-foot-tall brush, a bundle of blue bristles.

"That thing," I answer, "is a typewriter eraser."

"A what?"

"Do you know what a typewriter is?"

"Of course, it's like a computer, but prints directly on paper."

"Well, yes," I say, "but there's no 'delete' key to correct a mistake."

"Bummer."

"Yep, you have to roll the paper up a couple of clicks, and erase your mistake."

"How do you use that thing?"

I step over to the sculpture and place my hand on the pink disk. It feels like cold fiberglass, not the warm touch of soft rubber. "The actual typewriter eraser is only about three inches tall overall. The pink disk is soft rubber, about ⅛ inch thick. Just wide enough to rub out, or erase, one typed letter. The pink rubber contains a very fine abrasive that grinds away the typed error."

"Why the blue brush on top?"

"To brush away the debris after erasing," I say. "But most people just blew the stuff away. If the abrasive laden dust settled down into the delicate mechanism of the typewriter, it could cause damage for the life of the machine."

"Thanks," she says. "Thank God for evolution. I can type pretty fast, but I still make mistakes. The delete key is my savior. I would hate to have to use an eraser."

Today, thirty-five years after that encounter, I think about erasing my mistakes. It's not the same as deleting, where everything is gone. An eraser never quite removes all the memories of the mistake. The item may be gone, but a smudge is left on the page, along with the scattered physical remains. There's dust and abrasive from the worn eraser, along with the rubbed-out particles of the error scattered across the page. Where is the brush to finish?

Sometimes I wish time travel was possible. I would go back to an earlier date and shout at myself, "Don't marry that woman!" I would grab me and try to shake some sense into that twenty-year-old. "You're too young; it will not work. It won't last even eighteen months!"

But if I did go back, I didn't listen. That marriage and all the tag-along emotions have now been erased. However, some of the abrasive dust from that action have remained and cause damage in the present. Sometimes in the day-to-day, my perception is cloudy or dimmed and I make mistakes as foolish as did that twenty-year-old. I feel the remains, the dust and abrasive grit, and even bits and pieces that have been long ago erased grinding away at my here and now. I need a bigger, stiffer brush. Or better yet, a delete key.

Sometimes I feel like my life is being erased, bit by bit. It is not my hand on the eraser, but something else. I don't believe in a giant eraser in the sky held by an all-mighty hand. But what is it?

Many years ago, I joined the new tech world with a domain name, an email address, and a web site presenting my sculptures. It's all gone now but the memories.

My hands were the second to be erased. I can no longer hold a tool, I'm just barely able to clutch a stick to type one letter at a time on my keyboard. Memories. Often boring to everyone but myself. I try to tell a story to make the images more universal, better understood by a reader who could identify with the experience.

It's first light, the best time of the day. The deck is a good place for morning meditation, facing west and north. The bay waters are dark. The Marin shore to the north is even darker. Only the pale sky above the hills gives them definition. The morning breeze hasn't started. The sun has to heat the earth to create even a whisper of wind. Even so, the air carries a very faint, pleasing aroma. Somewhere, not far away, the earth is being awakened, being warmed. If I were a creator of women's perfume, I would create one appropriately called *First Light*.

A flash of yellow light leaps out from the dark hills to the north. Is it a fire? More points of light, some white, a few are red. Not a fire. These are the light refractions from a jewel. The hills begin to lose their darkness. The morning sun is peeking over the hills way to the east, behind me.

More light, more brilliant jewels flashing their lights to me. They are huge, as large as the windows of the houses that emit their brilliance. I am a wealthy man. I will carry these jewels with me today, out of reach of the eraser.

The trees on the hillside below me are dark, black shapes. Beyond and below them, a few gray spots move about. The sun continues its journey up, over the eastern hills. More light, more by the second. Trees become black/green, then green/black. The gray spots become white. Colors appear out of the semi-darkness. Color defines the shapes. The trees have dimension. The once gray-white spots moving below are workmen on a construction site wearing white hard hats.

The day has begun. The waters of the bay are shades of blue, depending on where the morning breeze has ruffled the surface. Sounds of construction drift up the hill. The trees are full of birds greeting the day in their own way.

A wealth of jewels has been safely stored in the pockets of my mind, far away, hidden from the eraser.

THE NAKED TRUTH

One day,

Dishonesty invited her twin sister Truth to go swimming.

Dishonesty had many names; Falsehood, Lie, Fake, Trumped-up, and many more. Truth was known as Honesty.

It was a beautiful warm sunny day, sunlight sparkled on the water. The two ran down to the water's edge.

Originally, as the story goes, the twins were swimming in a river. Always changing, always the same as the water flowed. Could this river have been the Euphrates where civilization emerged, or an even earlier river in Africa?

In the medieval version of the story, the twins swam in a well. At that time, rivers were filled with filth. A well was vital for the life of a community. A place to make wishes; the most frequent wish was that the bucket would be full of clean, clear water when winched up to the light.

It is easier to visualize the original river. The women disrobed, placing their garments on the low bushes growing along the banks. It felt good to be nude in the warm sun, the gentle breeze cooling their sensuous bodies. The twins enjoyed playing in the river, laughing and splashing. When her sister was not looking,

Dishonesty swam ashore, gathered up all their clothing, and disappeared.

Truth, coming out of the water and finding nothing to cover her body, was very distressed for now she was naked. From then on, humans had difficulty believing when Truth spoke because the words were not softened by the many layered folds of her beautiful garments. The people could only see the Naked Truth. Often it was not what they wanted to hear.

Meanwhile, Dishonesty would frequently dress in Truth's clothing. She appeared to be beautiful to many who looked and listened to her. When Dishonest spoke, people saw only the outer layers of Truth's garments; they believed the Lie which was being spoken, deceived into accepting it as the Truth.

The most egregious, the greatest lies coming from Dishonesty originate from the words and actions of those with power. The denial of civil rights, the rewriting of history, the ignoring of gun violence, and more. Perhaps the most serious example of looking away, of averting our eyes from the Naked Truth is the blindness to Her message about climate change.

This ancient, but timeless story needs to be told again and again. It is good to be reminded.

UPDATE

"Your wheelchair is worn out, you need an update."

My hands no longer worked on the push-rings of the mechanical wheelchair. It had been a mid-range purchase, but only two years old. I had thought I needed an add-on electric assist to help me maneuver. The wheelchair expert gave me the above diagnosis of my problem.

"In addition," the expert continued, "Your chair was never designed to be sat on for sixteen hours a day. No wonder it's worn out."

Originally, it had been difficult for me "updating" to a wheelchair. My first walking assist had been a tall staff. You know, like Gandalf. It was compatible with my white beard. All that was needed was a long, flowing robe to complete the image. Soon, I "updated" to two trekking sticks, a definite help with my balance as my legs grew increasingly numb. The next move was on to a four-wheeled walker, with a seat to use when I tired. My wife and I traveled to NYC and London. Restaurant and museum visits were a part of life. With the help of my studio assistant, I continued to sculpt. I could still hold a carving tool. I continued to drive…with the assist of hand controls for the throttle and brakes.

I have Amyloidosis, a hereditary disease. It attacks the body's nerves which control the movement of the muscles. It is a progressive disease. My legs were becoming increasingly numb. Someday, it will reach my heart, and I will die.

The image of using, of being confined to a wheelchair, grew stronger. This did not fit my self-image. I did not want to live my life in a wheelchair. I was ready to die, to cross over to the other side. Joining the non-physical world held no fear for me. In fact, I was very curious about what it would be like.

Shortly after my twelfth birthday, I became very sick. I died and crossed over. I arrived at a place that was very beautiful. When given the choice of staying or going back, I wanted to return. So now when confronted with the visual images of sitting all day long in a wheelchair, I chose to cross over.

But it did not happen. I talked with people who knew "how to" achieve end of life. I found a book on the subject. My business records were up to date. I asked my veterinarian if she could supply me with the right drug. (Sorry, no.)

It just didn't happen.

I don't know why. I found a doctor who knew about Amyloid. He said the prognosis for the disease was three to five years. I'm well ahead of the game, just waiting.

My current "update" is an electric wheelchair. It's very comfortable. I can sit all day, go out, go to dinner, (its foldable) and I realized that I'm in a much better place.

I don't know why, but my world is different now. I'm very aware of the slow, but steady decline in my physical abilities. However, my mind is still sharp enough. I can still clutch my typing stick to write. After dinner last night, I came to the realization that I was tired of almost (but not) dying. Every major purchase is shadowed with the question; will I live long enough to enjoy this item? It's been too many years, living on the edge of life not knowing when my update to the next world will happen.

I think that the recent update to my new wheelchair has given me a new view on life. A perspective to live life to the fullest. To push the outer limits. To explore a path not yet taken.

My latest update:

"Ain't dead yet!"

DARKNESS

It's dark, very dark. I don't know where I am. It's dark.

I try to remember. There is a terrifying tidal wave, stretching across the whole horizon. Everyone is running. Or was that just a dream? I'm in bed with a very nice, comfortable woman. Not a knockout beauty, but at my age, comfort is the best part of love-making. I'm hoping that was not a dream.

"Hello, anyone there?" I ask.

Silence, except for distant murmurs.

Darkness and silence…not a good combination. I'm not afraid. Just a feeling of unease. There is no light in the room, nothing to focus on. I feel dizzy, my head is spinning. I wonder if someone gave me a shot of something. I remember calling for help, maybe I was shouting.

Years ago, I hiked down into the Carlsbad Caverns in New Mexico. My Dad held my eight-year-old hand. The cave guide said the lights would be turned off for a few minutes. "No talking, hold on to someone. It will be so dark you can't see your hand in front of your face."

He was right. A few minutes passed, then out of the darkness and silence came a little voice, "Mommy, it's dark in here!" We all laughed, and the lights came on.

Where is my guide? Where is my mommy? Where is the light? I'm beginning to feel sensory deprivation. I recall the stories and studies that came out of the Korean War. There were accounts of torture using this technique. I am not afraid. But the unease is increasing.

There is no pain. That's the good news. Pain cannot be remembered. The incident of pain, the experience, the time and place can be recalled. But the feeling of pain itself cannot be remembered. I have experienced pain; some so intense I passed out. I am very relieved to be unable to re-experience those body-twisting extremes. I think I'm on drugs, a heavy dose of pain medication.

Am I dead? Have I crossed over? I don't think so. I do not believe in an "in-between place" of darkness. If I were dying, I should be following a light. This darkness is a totally new existence. There is no smell. Often there is a new smell with a new experience. The heavy sweet odor of flowers upon arriving in Hawaii. The dusty, delicious aroma of ripe, dry wheat ready for harvest. And of course, the salty fragrance arising from the wind-blown sea. Here there is nothing.

Could this be the physical setting of depression? I think not. For me, depression is a very low light. There is some light, but not enough to play in. It is not black, just dark. So where am I?

Depression is often accompanied by an uneasy feeling of emptiness. I feel alive, not vacant.

Is this the 'calm before the storm'? Maybe, but what storm? Looking over my life, I see no storm clouds approaching. Perhaps the storm is the ever-present process of aging. Not really a raging storm, but the increasing difficulty using my physical body. Oh, yes. My left arm…

Let's not go there.

Is it possible? The darkness is becoming darker as I think about the condition of my body. But where is the light? If I could just see a glimmer, a tiny pinpoint of light I could focus and move in that direction.

At age twelve, I died, crossed over, and returned. The existence, the presence of light, even just a speck of light, was and has been a comfort given to me on my adventure. Dying has been, for me, a subject of curiosity and excited expectation. But now this darkness has changed the parameters of the playing field.

I like Hunter S. Thompson's idea of what the end of life should be.

Life should not be a journey to the grave with the intention of arriving safely in a pretty and well-preserved body, but rather to skid in broadside in a cloud of smoke, thoroughly used up, totally worn out, and loudly proclaiming 'Wow! What a Ride!'
— Hunter S. Thompson

Accepting and embracing this darkness is the task at hand, just as accepting my hands as they are, unable to hold a sculpting tool, my fingers barely able to clutch a wooden stick to type with. And being regulated to a wheelchair.

Where are my other senses? They all seem to have been dampened or turned off. If I'm in a nursing facility, then it is just as well for the darkness of my senses. I don't have to hear the shouts and screams from down the hall. Or suffer the inhuman stench of my neighbor using a bedpan during the night. Even the rapped staccato footsteps in the hall are wrapped in this darkness.

Again, I say I'm not afraid. Just wondering how to get a grasp on what is happening. I close my eyes, thus shutting out the non-light. This closed eye darkness is now familiar.

Seeds of ideas, and scraps of dialogue swirl around in my thoughts, attempting to condense into recognizable, workable images. I am familiar, comfortable with this progress. This is creativity happening. When a seed (or a thought, or an image) is planted in the darkness, a gestation begins, and the new creation pushes itself into the light. This initial planting in the darkness is vital to the creative process.

In Greek mythology, the anthropomorphism of the darkness was represented by the god Hades, (not to be confused with the devil). Hades is Lord of the Underworld. He possesses all the earth's wealth and is the instigator of the creative process. He wears the helmet of invisibility, still, he remembers the light, guiding the seed, the thought to the light.

Years ago, participating in a guided meditation, I was directed to descend into the basement of my mind. From there on, I proceeded on my own. It was dark down there. A cord from an overhead light switch brushed against my face.

This meditation, this trip inward, came along at a time when I was questioning where to go with sculpting.

Pulling on the light cord, the basement room was flooded with light. In front of me were three sculptures, perfectly lit. Two were sculptures I had completed, and one I was working on. I stepped forward to touch the granite. The back wall of the room fell away, revealing many, many, maybe hundreds of finished sculptures. Walking out, touching the creations, each one came alive, became bathed, became infused with light.

I was in awe.

All I had to do was to do it.

A florescent light comes on overhead. I squint my eyes. The attendant opens the window curtains; morning light floods the room. Turning to me, she says, "Wake up, I'm going to take your vitals. You're going home today. Your wife's coming with your new wheelchair."

I try to remember where I am. Images streaming, fleeting across my mind. I try to interact with the memories. *What? Are you sure? Really?* None stop to answer.

Suddenly, my brain stops its scramble. Stabilized, not speeding past, but boldly offered are the words and memory, true today as they had been so many years ago:

All I have to do is to do it.

LAST DAY

Joe had been at his father's death bed…if one could expand the definition of 'death bed' to include the hours, even days before the actual crossing over. His mother had called Joe early in the morning to say that once again his father was in the ER. Joe had already made this trip four times in the past year, staying at the bedside, helping with the care of a dying old man. But each time, each visit, his father didn't die.

Joe caught an early flight to Seattle and went directly to the hospital. His father looked 'Like death warmed over.' His face was a colorless gray…a lifeless mask of the person Joe knew. An ill-fitting oxygen cup covered the mouth, and a pair of dirty eyeglasses blurred the eyes of the head sunk into the pillow. Joe removed and cleaned the eye ware. He asked his father if he really needed the oxygen and received a negative shake of the head.

Death hung in the air. There was a different, but distinct smell. It was not the repulsive odor of uncontrolled body waste, even though that was there also.

Joe knew his father was dying this time. Joe stood at the foot of the bed and asked his father if he could hear and see him. There was a definite nod. Joe told his father a joke about two men talking intently, neither understanding what the other was talking about.

When the joke was finished, his father's face registered a smile. Joe continued speaking, moving up alongside the bed.

"Dad," Joe said, reaching out to hold his father's hand. "You're dying. It's okay, it's time. You've had a good life. I know it's a frightening time, facing the unknown. If you need it, I'm giving you permission to cross over. I can help you with your journey."

Joe checked again to see if the older man was listening. "I've made this crossing myself, so I know the path," he said. "I came back, I was young and not ready to stay on the other side."

The older man's eyes remained focused on Joe.

"Follow the light," Joe said. "Some call it the 'Christ Light.' It will give you direction." Joe knew his father could relate to this religious language. "The Light is shining above on the inside of your forehead. Look up. Can you see it?"

The head shook 'No.'

"Keep looking," Joe said. "At first it may be just a faint glow. But as your vision adjusts, the light will become brighter."

Joe compared it to being out on a country road, on a dark night and seeing a farmstead's yard light in the distance, shining out across the prairie.

"I see it. I can really see the light! Oh God, there it is!" came the old man's affirmation.

Out of the corner of his eye, Joe noticed movement in the room. He glanced over, the doctor had come in. His mother, on the other side of the room, was motioning to the doctor to be quiet and not interrupt.

"When," Joe continued, "you're ready to start your journey, keep your eyes on the guiding light, keep going ahead. It's best not to look to the side, keep on the path."

Joe continued sharing with his father his own experience; the beautiful music, the gorgeous images, and the comforting presence that walked beside him. Joe could see his father's body relaxing, the pain subsiding.

"Dad, are you still awake? There's one more thing. A great philosopher (Joe didn't think his father could relate to the name Ram Das) once said that 'Death is the greatest adventure of all, that's why it's saved to last.' Dad, I love you," Joe said, squeezing the old hand. "Have a great, joyful, and wonderful adventure."

Joe had to leave to catch his flight home.

His mother called at 3:30 am. "Your dad was very relaxed after you left. He sent me home to get some rest. I met his doctor in the hall, he asked me to thank you for sharing 'travel plans' with him. He called me a few minutes ago and said your father had left to go on his last adventure."

Joe maneuvered his wheelchair to a larger sunny spot on the deck. The warmth felt good on his bare arms. This was his birthday month, the same month his father had died so many, many years ago. Perhaps that was why Joe had so vividly recalled his father's deathbed experience.

Joe's father died at age 77, his father before him had died at 67. Joe had often thought that he would live well into his 87th year. And his offspring even to 97. There was a good chance for that achievement. His mother lived well into her 94th year. Her parents reached 93 and 94.

But this month Joe would arrive at 84 years old. Three more years until 87 seemed a very long time, considering his life in a wheelchair, and the ongoing, incurable, life-threatening disease consuming his body.

Joe opened his eyes. He was cold. The sun was gone and the fog had silently snuck in. Time to go in. He must have fallen asleep. He seemed to be drifting off more and more often. Sometimes nodding out even in the middle of a thought or even a senten....

LIMINAL SPACE

That place between where you have been
and where you are going.

I am in that space now. It is uncomfortable. The realization that the substructure support I have built a life upon is no longer available.

"Who are you?" someone asks.

I can no longer answer that I am a sculptor, creating pieces from marble or granite, some as tall as eleven feet. I have given up what is known. My foundation, my very bedrock has been shattered. I am in an empty void.

The memories of the years before have begun to fade in intensity. The successes, the ones upon which I built my outer persona, have lost their brilliance. Shipping back twenty-ton containers of Italian marble. Six permanent sculptures in Manhattan, to mention a couple. Even the website of my sculptures has disappeared. Fortunately, the failures in life have also dimmed. A first marriage that lasted only a year. And...let's not go there.

This is a time of reduced perception. Weeks come and go. Sense organs are dulled. I need to check my phone to remember what day it is.

I remember my grandpa, sitting with his elbows on the table, staring. He had been a large, powerful man who built an empire on the prairie of western Kansas. That was in the early 1900s. Sixty years later, he was a little old man unable to work. He just stared, oblivious to the family bustle around him. Where was he going? What was he staring at? I wish I could have asked. But I was young then. There was enough momentum in my life to push through any liminal space, the betwixt and the between, and get on with the next involvement.

Was Grandpa remembering a previous time? Perhaps a time of liminal space when he abandoned the proven farming technique of driving a five pair team of mules, to be the first in his community to farm with a gasoline powered tractor. In the liminal space between the old and the new he must have been filled with both apprehension and excitement.

The bridles and other tack that had been used to harness the mules for work were still out in the barn, hanging on old nails. When the tractor took over their job, Grandpa did not sell the work animals. They were turned out to pasture, a field of nearly one hundred acres, to live out their lives. When the new tractor was working in the field next to the pasture, the old mules rushed to stand at the fence to remember and to watch the machine moving past, pulling a plow they had once pulled.

When entering into a liminal space, the past is only brought to mind to remember the old way. Going back is not an option; the past is over. The excitement, the possibilities, the promise of transformation are the pathway through the void. Focus on the new. Even though the future is unclear, it is the anticipation of the new, the "will be" that calms the apprehension.

I'm in that liminal space.

Memories of the past are fading. I've hung up my sculpting tools. Some are hanging on nails in the walls. A number of rough blocks of marble and granite wait quietly in the field next to my sculpting studio. Grass and weeds have grown around them and a tangle of blackberry vines cover their tops. All is silent, no sawing, no grinding, nor polishing noises emerge from the workplace. There's no echo from the staccato rhythm of hammer and chisel.

There is no stone dust in the air.

Tears come as I write this last paragraph, remembering. Knowing that I can never go back.

Cascade in Black and Light
12ft x 7ft × 2ft
Academy Black Granite, flowing water & fiber optic lighting

What is next? Sometimes I sit with my elbows on the table and gaze into the distance. Sometimes I wish I could have asked my grandpa what he could see. I see San Francisco Bay, the Golden Gate Bridge, and the sunset on the horizon out in the Pacific Ocean. Is that where I am going?

It is like being in a long corridor, barely lighted, with many doors lining the walls. The doors only have locks, no doorknobs. No way out, not even an "exit" sign. On the walls, dim pictures of the past; summer farm work, back-packing through Asia, dropping out of grad school, raising a child, twenty-plus boats I have enjoyed, fifty-plus years of a successful marriage, and sixty years sculpting. I keep walking. There must be an end to this pathway, even though it's not visible.

I approach a new, better-lighted picture. It could be a window. A glimpse outside and beyond the liminal space of the corridor. I look out (or in, or through). There I see myself, with a stick clutched in my bent fingers, typing on a keyboard. On a shelf above the computer monitor are books. The titles on two books, or is it three, are in sight…they are mine.

I feel energized. I want to shout. My heart is racing. I continue along the path. Where is this going? A smile stretches across my face. I am excited!

A vital memory, a vivid image jumps into my consciousness. Early in my sculpting career, while meditating, I counted down, down, down, down into the unknown darkness. I raised my hand overhead, found and pulled on a light switch cord. The whole room burst into light. Before me were three sculptures I had recently completed. Behind these three were more blocks of stone set on work stands, ready to be sculpted. The back wall of the room fell away, and as far as the eye could see, were stones (some very large) waiting be worked on. I knew I would never be without an image to be rendered, a sculpture to be created.

I am longing for that knowing, a life defined by creativity. The desire to get to work, to be creatively playful, to move beyond this restrictive tunnel of liminal space. Where is the end, the transformation?

There must be an exit, a way out to join the reality I viewed through the window. The corridor extends on before me. Is there something beyond my writing? Is there another reality beyond the thrilling creativity of organizing and placing thoughts and words on the page? I think I can feel the other side of this liminal space. I'm beginning to feel the return of emotions; the excitement of moving out of this space. Or is this just wishful thinking?

I lay my typing stick next to the keyboard. It's time for my lunch break. I will not sit with my elbows on the table, staring out at the bleak winter day. The morning fog is quietly disappearing. Maybe there will be sunshine this afternoon. I'll eat quickly and return to my creativity, my writing.

WHAT WILL BE

"Free at last, free at last," murmured Dr. Martin Luther King Jr. as he lay dying from an assassin's gunshot. I have thought about his last words often as I face my own end of life. I have lived long past the prognosis of my fatal disease.

When? How? Where? What will be?

Awaking from a late afternoon nap, I am cold. Too dizzy to sit up. "Is it now?" This question booms out from the thoughts rushing through my consciousness. The room is dark. My head spinning. Can't focus.

A dark, shade-like cloud moves over my eyes. Is this what my cardiologist meant telling me that someday my heart would slow, then stop? I close my eyes. In the darkness, I raise my eyes to search for the glowing light behind my forehead. This light will guide me on my journey.

I'm ready, but thirsty.

I don't want to cross over with a dry throat. Struggling to sit up, reaching for a mug of water…it's too full and too heavy. The cup slips. The water spills, soaking my shirt and the bed.

Wet and dizzy was not the way I had thought it would be when the time came. When I was twelve, I crossed over and came back. I recall, upon returning, a profound sense of peace that has enveloped me through the subsequent seventy-plus years of my life. At that time, I was not dizzy and wet, but I did leave from a physical state of great pain. The journey was beautiful, a wonderful experience. I have wanted to be involved in, and joyfully participating again in my next crossing over.

Now after a lifetime of study and meditation, I would like to be able to enjoy my final trip. Like Ram Das said, "Death is the greatest adventure of all. That's why it is saved to last."

I resist. I fight back against the spinning in my head. The bedroom is dark. Should I just lie back and go with the spin?

To be free…

"No!" I hear myself say. "I'm too thirsty."

Was this the human body's will to live? Even when standing on the edge of the greatest adventure, the body still wants to survive, to stay and …

My wife comes in and asks if I'm okay.

"I thought I was going," I say, struggling to sit up.

She helps me to a drink of water.

ACKNOWLEDGEMENTS

I want to thank my friend, mentor, teacher, and editor Tim Crandle for his continued guidance and encouragement. He helped me channel my creativity into words, a priceless gift at this stage in my life.

Thanks as well to my editor and writing coach Stacey Alysa Dennick.

ABOUT THE AUTHOR

Welton Rotz has been a sculptor of stone and metal, a blacksmith, a licensed a general contractor, a boat builder, and a teacher. In the early 1960s, he pursued graduate studies in Theology.

Disenchanted with church doctrine, Welton did not complete his degree, preferring to develop his spirituality through meditation, extensive research, and creativity. He went on to study psychotherapy.

Welton was born in 1940. At the age of nine, he lived with relatives on a wheat and cattle farm for six months before moving to the Philippines with his college professor parents. He learned to sail in Manila Bay. After four years overseas, Welton returned to the States. He spent every summer during high school and college farming with his uncle and cousin in western Kansas.

Sculpting and sailing have been his passion for many years.

In 2015 Welton was diagnosed with a rare, progressive amyloid neurological disease that severely impacted his hands and feet.

He lives in San Francisco with his wife Barbara Stuart and an Icelandic sheepdog named Mikilee. There, he types stories with a stick held between his bent fingers.

Heart of Lightness
10.5 ft tall, black granite & LED lighting

www.ingramcontent.com/pod-product-compliance
Lightning Source LLC
Chambersburg PA
CBHW051923240626
47153CB00004B/1345